Meg's
BEST MAN

Meg's BEST MAN

A MONTANA WEEKEND NOVELLA

By Cynthia Bruner

Meg's Best Man
A MONTANA WEEKEND NOVELLA

Cover by Robin Ludwig Design

Scripture taken from THE HOLY BIBLE, NEW INTERNATIONAL VERSION®, NIV® Copyright © 1973, 1978, 1984, 2011 by Biblica, Inc.® Used by permission. All rights reserved worldwide.

ISBN: 978-0-9862153-1-5

Meg's Best Man is a work of fiction. References to real people, events, establishments, organizations, or locales are intended only to provide a sense of authenticity and are used fictitiously. All other characters, incidents, and dialogue are drawn from the author's imagination.

Printed in the U.S.A.

Thursday Night

It was exactly the wrong time to show up at Joshua's cabin. The would-be bride's face was wet with tears, and her future father-in-law was pacing with one palm pressed to his forehead. Her future mother-in-law was sitting beside her, holding her hand. "It'll work out, dear," she was saying. Leah, the would-be bride, made an attempt at a hopeful smile. It didn't work. Then, because she was trying not to cry, a sob leaked out and made an awful squeaking sound.

That sent the groom over the edge. "I know they have antinausea medications. Have they given her any? Why isn't she better yet? I need to talk to that doctor." With that, Joshua started pacing around the cabin's great room, looking a lot like his father, who had already started to wear down the wooden floor.

Meg obediently closed the front door of the cabin behind her, wishing her aunt hadn't said "Come in" a few moments before. What was this about nausea? Leah looked distressed, not sick. Meg looked at her cousin Joshua as he stomped around in a blur. He was definitely not sick, but he could end up that way soon if he kept this up.

Aunt Catherine turned and gave Meg a bright smile,

as if nothing was wrong. "Come in," she said again. "It's so good to see you, Meg."

Leah took a shaky breath. "I'm sorry," she croaked, wiping her eyes with her sleeve.

"Is there something I can do to help?"

The sudden end to the stomping caught her attention, and Meg looked up to see her cousin staring at her, his gray eyes wide and his mouth half open. He nodded quickly and mouthed yes. Then he glanced at his fiancée as if he was afraid she would see him.

She felt a touch on her arm and turned to Aunt Catherine, who was gently pulling her down to sit next to her. "We just got word that Brie, who is Leah's maid of honor, has a severe case of food poisoning. She missed her flight, and the doctor doesn't think she'll be well enough to fly before the wedding on Saturday. We came up to give Leah the bad news."

Now she understood why her aunt and uncle were at the cabin tonight, rather than hosting the flock of Parks family members down at their own house. There was no phone service at the cabin, where Leah and Joshua were staying. There was a spot a quarter mile up the mountain on a rocky outcrop where you could make a call if you held your cell phone up in the air, but if there was a message to deliver, it had to come in person.

Meg looked at Leah. Leah managed to make crying look pretty, except for the runny nose. "Can one of the other bridesmaids step in?"

Leah shook her head a little. "There's just Brie and Cadence." Cadence was Joshua's little sister, and although she could be charming, Cadence was nineteen and spent a lot of time in her own boy-chasing little world, oblivious to anyone else's needs. She wouldn't make the best maid of honor.

"Do you have any other friends coming?" As soon as she saw the tears start to pool, Meg wished she hadn't asked that. Brie had probably been the only one. Leah was from Texas, and it was a long, expensive trip. The nearest hotel to the cabin was an hour away. Some people didn't mind camping, but it was a lot to ask. Besides, Meg realized, it was awfully late in the game to get someone else to fly up north just to be a backup. Leah was truly in a bind.

Movement down the hall caught Meg's attention, and she could see someone in the shadows. A man, a tall one, was leaning sideways against the wall. He looked awfully comfortable in Joshua's cabin, and she wondered who he was and what on earth he was doing there. He certainly wasn't helping anyone. Meg felt Joshua's eyes on her again, and she looked up to see the intensity on his face. She suddenly understood what he was waiting for. He wanted her to be the maid of honor.

Her head started to hurt. This weekend was going to be her only weekend off in two months. She had pulled her camper up here, and she was going to split her time between seeing family and reading a book or seven. She was only here now, standing in this cabin, to be polite and let Joshua know she'd be parking the camper down on the old logging road.

Leah was fidgeting with a wet tissue and let out another squeak. It was clear her mother wasn't in Montana yet, or else she would be here now. And her sister wasn't here, unless she was hiding in a back room. Meg vaguely remembered that she was out of the country. Now Leah's best friend wasn't coming.

Last December, just after Joshua had asked her to marry him, Leah had spent Christmas at Aunt Catherine and Uncle Jacob's place. Meg had been there too, and the two of them had spent a lot of time together. Meg liked Leah. She liked her cheerful determination, even though she was a city girl in a house full of Montana loggers, cowboys, and refinery workers. She was looking forward to spending time with her again, but she was not Leah's *best* friend. As she watched her shred the poor tissue, it came to her that she was probably the best friend Leah had in Montana. She reached over to the table, pulled out a couple clean tissues, and then handed them to Leah.

Without looking, Leah grabbed the tissues and dumped the sopping, shredded one in Meg's open hand. A split second later she realized what she had done and looked at Meg with wide eyes. "Oh! I'm so sorry . . ."

Meg laughed and handed it to Joshua as he passed by in his pacing. "Better get used to this," she said to him with a laugh. "Wet tissue holder will be part of your job description."

Meg turned back to Leah. "I'm sorry, Leah. I know you were counting on your friend being here. There's still a chance, isn't there? But if Brie doesn't make it, you've got a whole bunch of Parks girls, including me, who would be honored to step in. You should just pick one who fits in the dress and put them to work." And hopefully, she thought, it will be one of the others.

Leah took a deep breath and looked at her with pleading eyes. "Would you? Do you really mean it?"

Uh-oh. "I do." Yikes, that sounded like a vow, Meg thought. What did maids of honor do, anyway? She'd have to ask Aunt Catherine. No one was better at coordinating events than her. She probably already had a list prepared.

"Oh, the dress! What if it doesn't fit you?"

Meg's head pounded now. She had a dress for the

wedding, one she really liked, but she would probably wear jeans and a nice blouse instead. She really wasn't the dress kind of girl, and a cabin in the woods wasn't much of a high-heels place, anyway. Leah always looked so put together, accessories and all, so it was probably going to be a fancy bridesmaid outfit. Oh please, God, she thought, I want to be a friend for Leah, but please don't make me wear dyed-to-match shoes. I really don't like dyed-to-match shoes. "We'll figure that out later."

"Let's go try it on now," Aunt Catherine said, taking her hand. "Come on, Meg, this way."

Leah gave Meg a real smile. Joshua had stopped pacing, and so had his father, Meg's Uncle Jacob. They were all looking at her with hope in their eyes. All except for the lanky cowboy lurking in the back hallway, that is, who had an inscrutable grin on his face. Who let him in, anyway?

Catherine led her down the opposite hallway to the cabin's main bedroom and opened the door. There was some nice luggage in the corner. Meg guessed it was where Leah was staying. There were three dresses hanging over the front of the wardrobe: a wedding dress, a nice blue dress, and a brilliant Kelly green halter dress. Catherine reached for the green one. Tucked against the wall was a strappy pair of matching shoes.

Not much got past Aunt Catherine. "Thank you, Meg. I know this isn't your style, but it will mean the world to Leah. Do you know she hasn't got a single friend coming up from Texas now? Her friends Marci and Nan just started new jobs and couldn't take time off. Besides, as you know, this place isn't on the way to anything those girls would find exciting. I'm just grateful Gage is here for Joshua." She set the dress down on the bed. "I'll be back to zip you up in a moment," she said and she closed the door behind her.

Meg stripped down to her socks and underwear and put on the dress. She was hoping it would either fit perfectly or fit so badly that she wouldn't have to wear it, but neither was the case. It seemed a little longer than it was supposed to be, and it was tight enough across her bust that it gaped in the front, showing off the edge of her bra when she moved. She tried on the shoes, and thankfully they didn't even come close to fitting. Catherine came back in and stood before her, hands on hips. "Well, you'll have to wear different shoes. Now just look at that face! You look like you don't care for it, and you haven't even seen how it looks yet."

"It's bright."

"All your murals have bright colors, Meg. I never understood that. Why is it you never dress yourself like you do your artwork?"

Well, that was an interesting question, but she wasn't about to address it now.

Catherine moved the blue dress, revealing the mirror on the front of the wardrobe. Then she physically moved Meg over in front of it. "You don't usually show that much skin, I know," she said. "I wish you'd give my Cadence a good dose of your natural modesty; she could use it these days. Hers is the same color of green and has short sleeves, and she'd trade dresses with you in a heartbeat. And no, you may not suggest it." She untied and retied the halter at the back of Meg's neck, which helped a little. "It's a little bit . . ."

"Busty," Meg finished. "And it's me, not the dress."

Catherine laughed. "There's nothing at all wrong with your figure, missy, you're a bombshell. I'm quite sure the gentleman you marry won't mind that at all."

Meg felt embarrassed and fussed at her waist. "It's

tight here, too."

"Well, Brie is a twig. I know you think it's too flashy, but the truth is, you look lovely."

Meg tilted her head sideways and gave herself a critical look in the mirror. "It's just a little too tight. It makes the dress look . . . inappropriate."

Catherine laughed. "I knew you were going to think that. If you knew Brie you'd realize she sees this dress as too plain. The truth is somewhere in between. It's just for one day, anyway."

"Ah, but the pictures live on forever."

Catherine laughed again. "Come on, Meg. You have to give a fashion show now, goofy wool socks and all."

She hoped Leah would be happy. Joshua would be happy if Leah was happy, and if Joshua was happy, his mom and dad and even she would be, but . . . "Aunt Catherine, who is that guy out there?"

"The handsome stranger in the cowboy hat? It's about time you asked. That's Gage, Joshua's best man. I'm guessing he's going to like the dress, too."

If he did, he didn't give any indication of it. He had moved out of the hallway and into the great room, but he was still silently leaning against the wall like some sort of western decoration. The sun was starting to set outside, and the light was turning gold. Through the window it struck his tan skin and amber eyes. He looked as if he'd just come in off the range. Yes, he was handsome, but he was also a stranger, and she felt so awkward in her tight dress and gray wool socks she wanted to crawl into a hole.

Leah jumped up. "Oh, Meg, you look great!" What followed was a loud consensus on how great she looked, minus any opinion from Gage, the best man. Catherine broke the news to Leah about the shoes, but Leah didn't seem to mind at all. She gave Meg a surprisingly strong hug. "You're the best," she said.

"Well, I don't even know how to be a bridesmaid, let alone a maid of honor, so I hope I don't mess it up."

Aunt Catherine stepped up, as expected. "When things go wrong at the last minute you take care of everything and never let the bride know about it. And you stay by her side as much as you can, and if she tries to make a break for it, tie her down." Leah and Joshua exchanged a look that made it clear she wouldn't be going anywhere.

Meg went back to the bedroom to change into her own clothes and boots. When she came out her aunt and uncle were saying their good-byes. "I should go, too," she said. "I need to get the camper parked before dark, and I think there's some brush to clear on the lower logging road."

"You can't do that by yourself!" Catherine said. Then she glanced over at Gage.

Oh, no, Meg thought. That was just what she needed, her very determined aunt trying to do some matchmaking. "I can and I do, all the time," she said. "I spend more time on location than I do in my apartment, Aunt Catherine. I've got it covered." Then, hoping she had put a period on the end of that sentence, she added, "Are Mom and Dad at your place yet? Say hi for me, will you?"

After Aunt Catherine and Uncle Jacob left, Meg made sure she understood tomorrow's plans and gave Leah a last hug. Everyone seemed happy and relaxed. But almost as soon as the door closed behind her, it opened again. "I should help you get set up," Gage said, following her.

He didn't say he wanted to, or ask if he could help,

he just informed her that he should. And he didn't look too sure about it. She turned to face him and crossed her arms. "I really am fine," she said. "Please don't feel like you need to help; there's nothing to help *with*."

Gage walked right past her, and she had to look up as he did. He was taller up close. And he smelled like a very nice aftershave. "Nice canned ham," he said.

He meant her old-style little camper, of course. She loved it. It was tiny, round, and flat on the sides like a canned ham tipped on its side. It was also light enough to be pulled by a station wagon, or in her case, a Jeep. He walked right up to her Jeep and opened the passenger door. "Don't worry, I'll just walk back up to the cabin." Then he started to get in.

He must have noticed the shocked look on her face, because he jumped back out. She expected him to apologize and go back inside the log cabin, but instead he hurried around the front of the Jeep and opened her door. Then he actually took off his hat. And smiled.

It was one of those smiles, the kind that are usually part of an invitation to do something that will get you in trouble. She almost wanted to smile right back at him, but Meg knew better than that. She stepped off the front porch and came around to the driver's side. He stretched out one arm to welcome her into her own vehicle. It would have been a polite gesture if he hadn't invited himself along.

"Thank you," she said as she climbed into the driver's seat, "but I don't really need any help."

"No problem." He put his hat back on, got in the passenger side, slammed the door shut, and made himself comfortable. When she didn't make a move, he turned to her in surprise and added, "Oh, should I help you get this thing turned around?"

She didn't have anything polite to say to that. Frustrated, she cranked the ignition and started to back up the rig. She had to calm herself a little bit. If she wasn't careful she could turn the Jeep too tightly and bang the back corner of the Jeep into the camper. There were at least three paint swipes on the camper that demonstrated how she'd learned that lesson.

Once she'd turned the rig around, she started down the steep road in first gear. The camper didn't weigh much, but the Jeep wasn't really made to tow. She was thinking about how she was going to get onto the old logging road. The only way that made sense was to pass it, then back the camper onto the narrow road. It would make getting out a lot easier, but it was going to take some gas to get the old Jeep to shove the camper uphill, and backward, for a few feet. The Jeep wasn't what it used to be, thirty years ago.

As she crept past the turn for the logging road, she noticed a large branch across it. She should have checked the old road on the way up to the cabin, but she'd been anxious to get situated. And now that it was late, it was getting harder to see, and she had to park the camper. She put on the brakes and got out to put rocks in front of the tires just in case. She heard Gage jump out of the Jeep and head down the road. "It's been a while since someone drove down this road, huh?" he yelled cheerfully.

Once she was sure her rig was safe, she walked around the back and headed down the abandoned road. Gage was reaching down for the branch. "I'll get that," she said. She was irritated at herself for not taking care of this before, and that irritation was coming out in her voice.

Gage backed off, both hands raised, and she reached

down.

The branch didn't budge. It didn't look that heavy, but it was dead solid. She knew at first touch she was going to have to ask for his help, but she kept trying to move it. Finally, she looked up. It was getting dark fast, and she'd better admit defeat.

"I can't move it."

"You don't say."

"Would you please be so kind as to help me?"

Gage walked over behind her back, up onto the slope, and started tugging hard at another branch. It had pinned down the one that lay across the road. She hadn't taken the time to size up the situation, but evidently he had. With the other branch moved, the two of them were able to move the branch that blocked the road.

They walked together down the old logging road, each one in a tire rut, kicking their way through the tall grass and moving rocks and branches. They made it to a nice level spot that was well hidden in the trees, and she put her hands on her hips and looked around. "This looks great," she murmured to herself. She kicked off the extra branches and rolled a stone farther down the road. She could hear Gage walking back to her rig, but she had no idea how far he'd made it until she heard the unmistakable rasping roar of the old Jeep's engine.

"Wait!" she called and started running, but it was too late. Hitting RPMs the engine hadn't hit in years, her camper bounced up and over the hump where the two roads met and rocked perilously side to side. Then the rig was fully on the logging road, the engine was still running, and Gage jumped out looking proud of himself. "How far back do you want it?"

She resisted the urge to say she wanted it parked over his dead body, even though it seemed like an appropriate thing to say at the time. He hadn't exactly committed car theft, but he was at least rude. "I've got it from here," she said calmly.

He shrugged and held the door open for her. And took his hat off again. Maybe it was the color of the straw cowboy hat, but she had assumed he was blond, so the shock of dark hair—black in this dim light— surprised her again.

Once she was in, he slammed the door. She looked at him in surprise, but he was smiling. He looked to be around thirty years old, but he still seemed to think that was the normal way to close a car door.

"I'll be fine," she said through the plastic window and started backing up. But instead of heading back up the drive, he strolled after her, lit by the headlights as she backed up through what looked like a pitch-black tunnel in the rearview mirror.

It was slow going, but she got it parked. She dropped the hitch jack, and without a word Gage moved the Jeep out of the way. She pulled four jacks and a flashlight out of the bumper box, and by the time she had finished placing one he had done the other three, letting her know all the while what the level indicators were saying. The whole process was done in a flash, and she even got the propane pilot lit without its usual stubbornness and sputtering.

It would have been a good note to end the evening on, but Gage just kept going. While she was on the other side of the trailer she heard the step being pulled out, and he opened the door to her camper. "Hey," she called, but he didn't stop. As she rounded the other side, she saw the light come on in the camper.

"It's Mouse!"

Meg stopped in her tracks, eyes closed, and wished

again he would have just let her be. And she wished he had said, "It's a mouse," but she knew he hadn't.

He popped his head out of the doorway. "Why do you have Mouse the Moose all over your walls?"

"I think he's cute," she said.

He vanished again. "This is all painted directly on! Didn't Catherine say you were a painter? Did you paint all these?"

She nodded, knowing full well he couldn't see her.

He popped out again, eyes wide. "Did you write the book?"

"Yes. But could you please not tell . . ."

He was gone again. "This is awesome! My nephew would go crazy about this. It's his dream come true, camping with Mouse the Montana Moose."

She stepped up into the camper. There was only about six square feet of floor space, and Gage was taking up most of it, with his head tilted sideways not to hit the ceiling. *He doesn't fit in here*, she thought.

There wasn't much empty wall space, but she had managed to cover almost all of it with mountain scenery, wild animals, and Mouse the Moose sweetly and blissfully getting in trouble. It made her smile. And when she met with clients in her camper, which was not exactly the best business office, it instantly put them at ease. She backed her way into the narrow seat at her tiny table.

"'Mouse was a very good moose,'" he said. "'It was his antlers that were naughty from time to time. And the problem with antlers is that you can't act like they don't belong to you.'" He laughed. "I love that!"

He was quoting her own children's book, apparently by memory. It made her stomach do flips and her head hurt in a way that wasn't all bad.

"My nephew Cade makes me read your book over and over, and he says I have the best Moose voice ever. Do you have any other books out?"

"My publisher wants to do another, and I've been working on a few ideas."

"That's great. You'd better get on it so I can buy it for Cade for Christmas and cement my place as Uncle of the Year. I can't believe Josh never told me you were the author. The book says Margaret Parks, doesn't it? I never thought to make the connection; Parks is a pretty common name. Still, I can't believe—"

"He doesn't know."

Gage was perfectly still. His pale brown eyes pierced her. "Why not?"

"I guess I never got around to telling them," she said weakly.

Gage was frowning, now. She didn't know him from Adam, but that look made her feel as low as dirt. "'Them?' Does that mean no one in your close-knit, loving, good Christian family knows? Do your parents even know?"

She shook her head. Then she concentrated very hard on knitting her fingers together. *I'm scared to tell them*, she thought, but she didn't say anything.

Gage huffed. "Well, don't worry. I won't let your little secret out. I won't even tell Cade about it, even though I know he'd love to see some pictures of your camper, and he'd think I was especially cool for having met you, but I'm sure you have your reasons."

His expression made it clear he thought her reasons must be selfish. He tipped his hat and left.

She was still for a moment, but with a jolt that left her heart racing she jumped up and out of the cabin. "Gage!" she called.

He was just a little ways down the road, but she could make him out in the fading light as he turned to face her. He waited for her to say something. It shouldn't matter to her what he thought of her. She shouldn't have to defend herself to him. She tried to think of something else to say.

"Do you have any bear spray?"

"No."

"Do you have a gun?"

"The airlines frown on carrying a gun on the plane."

She smirked in the dark. "Let me get you some bear spray. I have plenty." She ducked back inside and fished through one of her tiny cabinets, which was a hopeless jumble now, and pulled out a huge black can. When she turned around he was standing right in the doorway and she jumped.

"I'm not a bear," he said calmly.

"You need to know how to use this."

"I know how," he said and removed it from her hand.

"Do you use it on wild bears roaming the streets of Austin?"

He grinned again, finally, and she felt so relieved she almost giggled. "You'd be surprised," he said, and with another tip of his hat he was gone.

Friday

Meg put the percolator over the blue gas flame. It was June, but the mountain night had been cold, and she was looking forward to a hot mug in her hands. Perked coffee and boiled water were the only things she made on the two-burner stove top of her camper, since cooking smells lingered forever in the small space. Coffee first, clothes second. She thumbed through her Bible until the coffee was ready. This particular Bible lived in her camper, and it looked worse for the wear. She wondered what God thought about years' worth of coffee drips and rings on His book and hoped He didn't mind too much.

She put on board shorts, a swim tank, and a camp shirt and added a pair of water shoes to her messenger bag. Sitting on the table, only slightly battered from the beating it had taken on its journey onto the logging road, was a large wrapped present. It was probably too early to bring that up to the cabin. Of course it was a framed picture, there was no hiding that. She'd tried to make up for the lack of surprise by making the package a colorful explosion of ribbons and sparking confetti paper.

I never understood why you don't dress yourself like

you do your artwork, Catherine had said. She looked at her pale blue shirt and black and brown plaid shorts. They were kind of surfer/boarder chic, weren't they? Or did they just make her look like a middle-aged man? She sighed. Well, they were comfortable. Luckily it was Leah who would be the center of attention today, not her. Everyone looking at one of her murals made her feel wonderful. Everyone looking at *her* made her feel awkward.

She threw a few more odds and ends in the bag and headed out to do her usual campsite check, but when she opened the door she found Gage standing still with his arm raised to knock on the door. She jumped backward so far she almost fell into the mini bathroom.

"I'm still not a bear," he said. "Sorry. Hey, is that coffee I smell? Do you have any more?"

"What are you doing here?" Her words sounded much harsher than she intended. "It isn't time for the rehearsal breakfast, is it?"

"No, I just thought I'd walk you up to the cabin. I do have the bear spray," he said, holding his trophy up in the other hand. The can's safety band was still in place.

"I have more," she said, meaning bear spray.

"Great, I'd love some coffee!" he said and stepped up into the cabin. He closed the door behind him. "It's nice and warm in here. It's pretty cold out until you get up into the sunshine."

She pulled a second mug from her cabinet. He peered over his shoulder, head held sideways because his hat couldn't clear the ceiling. "Hey, don't those things break in there, all tossed in like that? I would've guessed you had to organize them so they don't bang into each other."

She took a slow breath. "Everything got messed up

on the way in here." *When you backed up the camper like a BMX rider going up a ramp, that is.*

"Guess that's one of the hazards of moving your home from place to place."

She gave him a blank look. "Milk?"

"No thanks. This isn't one of those flavored coffees, is it?"

"Yes, it is."

He shrugged. "Still tastes fine. Thanks." With that Gage sat down, leaving his long legs in the tiny hallway, and removed his hat. He looked like he planned to stay a while. He glanced over at her Bible. "So, are you a . . ."

"Jesus freak? Mm hmm."

He looked relieved. "I don't know what to call it, or if it's okay to ask. It feels kind of like asking what brand of underwear you wear or something, like it's too personal. Do I say Christian or something else?"

She had to think about that. "I guess most of the people I run into ask if you're a believer."

"Wasn't there a song about that in the movie *Shrek*? I'm a believer."

Meg laughed. "I don't think that's what the song was about. So, are you a believer?"

He nodded. He looked like he was going to say more, but instead he downed the rest of the coffee and stood up as straight as he could. "Leah's got breakfast going. Joshua bought a new grill for her, and she's going to town on it."

"Joshua is up?" Meg said.

"Oh, no. But he will be when he gets a whiff of what she's cooking."

When they made it up the long road to Joshua's cabin, they saw Leah cooking over a huge, shiny new barbecue grill. Leah waved her spatula at them. "French toast is almost done. Which one of you has the dangerous job of waking my fiancé?"

Meg raised her hand. "I'm a pro," she said. She had spent most of the summers of her youth, and a few stray winters, living with Aunt Catherine and Uncle Jacob. Joshua's love of sleep was well known. The trick to waking him was to get out of the way.

She started with a mug of coffee, with milk, half-full so he wouldn't spill it. Then she slowly opened the big bedroom down the other hall from Leah's room, but she found it empty—and decorated with flowers. She smiled. That was probably Catherine's doing. That left the boys' bunk room as the only place for the men to sleep. She was extra careful opening the door because he might be within striking distance.

Lucky for her he wasn't just on the other side of the room, he was on one of the top bunks, snoring away. She first blew over the top of the coffee to carry the scent into the room. "Joshua, coffee," she whispered. "Coffeeeeee."

He grumbled something unintelligible.

She grabbed a pillow and tossed it. The first shot missed, but she grabbed another and scored a direct hit onto his head. He growled and his fists went flying through the air, hitting nothing. Then he ducked under the covers again. "Coffee, Josh," she sang.

Grumble. "Cream?"

"Milk."

Grumble. She crept into the room. One of Joshua's arms reached out. She carefully placed the mug in his hand, and then it disappeared under the covers by his head. She heard a loud sip.

When she turned around she saw Gage in the doorway, shaking his head. She was headed his way

23

when she heard a telltale rustle behind her, and without looking she ducked low. A pillow flew over her head and hit Gage directly in the stomach.

"Hey!" Gage yelled.

"Some best man you are. You're supposed to defend me. Who let the morning person in here?"

Meg tried to grab the pillow out of Gage's hands, but he held tight. "He didn't just let me in, he came and got me. He must know what a grump you are. I'd better warn Leah not to marry you."

Joshua was a bed-headed, swollen-eyed mess. "What is wrong with you people? And what is that incredible smell?"

"Leah's breakfast," Gage said. "I'm not guaranteeing that anything will be left if you keep lounging around in bed."

Meg slipped out the door, and Gage closed it behind her. He was a little too close and a little too tall, and she found herself staring at the spot between his collarbones. He was in her way.

There was that nice smell again. How did he pull that off? There were no showers at the cabin, only the water spigot outside and the river down in the valley. Just before she decided to crawl out of the way, he moved and let her pass. She thought she heard him chuckle. She sure hoped he was laughing at Joshua and not her, because she didn't want him to know he was bugging her. He seemed to thrive on it, and she had learned on the playground decades before that the best way to get rid of that kind of boy was to ignore him.

"Did you hear if Mark was coming?" Leah asked, switching from one cast-iron pan to another.

"I don't think so." And without Internet access she wouldn't know until her brother either arrived or didn't.

Leah didn't seem bothered by his lack of RSVP. Mark was pretty well known for not keeping in touch, but he was seventeen, after all.

The big table on the deck was set, there were wildflowers in a mason jar, and there was enough food to feed an army. It felt like Sunday brunch at Catherine and Jacob's house, and Meg loved it. The water pitcher with a filter in it was new. It seemed like a good idea, but she'd grown up drinking this water right out of the ground. Everything looked great. But Leah's forehead was all wrinkled up, and there was a frenzied quality to the way she was working.

Sliding up beside her, Meg helped move some of the serving plates over to the table. "You're not supposed to be working hard today, Leah. Please give me something to do."

"I just want it all ready before she gets . . . before they all get here."

As far as Meg knew, the only people coming were Aunt Catherine and Uncle Jacob, Meg's own parents, Uncle Jeffrey, Joshua's brother and sister, and Leah's mom. She guessed Leah was talking about either Catherine, her future mother-in-law, or Leah's own mom. It seemed likely that it was one of them who would have the power to make her so nervous. "It looks so pretty, Leah. I've never seen the deck look this good. And I saw the white ribbons and cloth in the cabin; I can't wait to get it all up so we can see it ready to go. It's almost like decorating for Christmas."

"It's a lot to get done," Leah said, flipping another batch of French toast in the cast-iron griddle.

"I'll get it done, don't worry. And by this afternoon there will be a ton of other people here who want to help, too."

Leah's shoulders dropped, and she looked up from the grill and out over the valley below. "It's still not going to be okay. I know Catherine went to so much trouble to make her feel at home, but she's used to big, fancy hotels and concierge service, and she hates bugs and ground that scuffs her shoes and well water . . ."

That explained which mom, and the water filter. Meg put an arm around Leah's shoulders. "That's going to be really hard. I know you like it here, and I bet you wish she did too."

Leah nodded silently.

"Leah, the good thing is Joshua's here, and he loves you more than anything in this world. Try to remember it's all about you two now. It's about all of us blessing your marriage. It's about you and Josh blessing each other. And anyone who is cranky, puking, wimpy, or whatever just shouldn't matter this weekend."

Leah snickered. "You have a way with words, Meg. You should be a writer."

She might have told Leah about her book right then if Gage and Joshua hadn't walked out onto the deck. Joshua looked awful. She glanced at Leah, who was looking at him like he hung the moon, and smiled. It made her feel funny, the way they couldn't see anyone else. She felt like an intruder, and she was happy for them. And she was a little bit jealous of their relationship.

Not that she would have any idea what to do with a husband, anyway.

They all heard the sound of an engine at the same time, and Jacob and Catherine's blue Expedition drove into sight. Before the engine was off, her aunts, uncles, and two of her cousins poured out. She waited. There was no sign of her parents. And with a quick glance at

Leah she confirmed that there was also no sign of Leah's mother.

There was a flurry of hugging and loud back slapping as Uncle Jeffrey greeted Joshua. "I can't tell you what it means to me to be here, Josh! What a blessed time this is." He then turned toward the girls. He looked like a taller, thinner version of her own father. "Leah! It's so good to see you again." He rushed over and gave her a hug and a back slap that sounded a little painful. If it hurt, Leah kept it to herself. Meg was next. It didn't hurt that badly, that was just Uncle Jeffrey. She wondered if he gave the same thumping hugs to the elderly ladies in his congregation.

Catherine made her way over, and she took Leah's hand with a gentle look on her face. Meg braced herself for bad news. "Brittany is going to come in on the first plane tomorrow morning, Leah. She had a little difficulty finding accommodations, and she didn't want to trouble me by staying at our place."

There was no way that the hotels in the valley were full, Meg thought. That only happened on rodeo weekend. Besides, Bozeman was little more than an hour away. Weren't there plenty of rooms there? "Yeah, well," Leah said. "It's very kind of you to say that, Catherine. She didn't need to be here for the rehearsal, anyway. She had already told me she didn't want to walk me down the aisle. She said it would make her feel old."

"Oh, honey," Catherine said. "I'm so sorry."

Leah nodded.

Catherine turned her gentle look on Meg. "Meg, your parents had some business in Billings today. They're working on transporting some clothing to Burma for a nonprofit there. They thought they might make it back in time for dinner, though." Meg smiled and nodded.

They wouldn't make it, of course. She tried not to let it set her on edge. After all, she would be around all weekend, and their latest project might not.

"Well, is anyone hungry?" Leah asked.

Meg was finally put to work filling up plates and setting them in front of her aunts, uncles, and cousins, and one strange Texan. When she could finally sit down she realized how tough it all must be on Leah. None of these people were her family. She fit right in, though. And so did Gage, she realized, as he seemed to have everyone around him laughing about something.

Her uncle Jeffrey quieted his own raucous laugh and stood up. "Let's say grace." It only took about three lines. She decided he'd given his abbreviated breakfast version. Either that or the smell of bacon, eggs, French toast, biscuits, and orange juice were getting to him, too.

It was a long meal, with everyone eating too much and talking too long. They finally got around to deciding where the chairs would go, where the aisle would be, and when Leah would come out into the little meadow in front of the cabin, and the official rehearsal began.

For some reason it never occurred to Meg that she would have to walk down the aisle with Gage. They had to leave first, being the best man and the honorary maid of honor. He held his arm out for her, she placed her hand in the crook of his arm, and he placed his other hand over hers. She was pretty sure he wasn't supposed to hold her hand like that, but it felt comfortable. They parted ways near Uncle Jeffrey.

Next were Joshua's brother and sister, Caleb and Cadence. Cadence was wearing a tube top over a string bikini and short shorts. Meg remembered what Catherine had said, something about Cadence needing a dose of modesty. When you're nineteen and pretty, it's hard to remember that someone else's wedding rehearsal isn't the best place to dress for attention.

But if the truth was told, Meg envied Cadence's slim body. Most of all, she envied what seemed to be her absolute comfort inside that skin. At nineteen, all Meg had ever worn was baggy jeans and hooded sweatshirts.

Meg suddenly had an idea for another Mouse the Montana Moose character—an animal who wore extra fur because she didn't like her own. Or maybe she wore moose antlers because they made her feel pretty. Meg could see the images forming in her mind's eye, and she almost missed the fact that Leah was walking down the imaginary aisle.

When Jeffrey got to a summary of the vows, both Joshua and Leah got giggly. Then Uncle Jeffrey started snickering. This could make for an entertaining ceremony, Meg thought. She glanced sideways and caught Gage staring at her. He wasn't laughing, he was just staring. It made her feel so awkward that she had to look away. Was she doing something wrong? Fly undone? A bug in her hair?

As soon as the rehearsal was over, they all got busy decorating. Swags of cloth and white solar Christmas lights went everywhere. Meg had plenty of ideas, and Leah had a good critical eye. With two ladders and willing workers, they managed to turn the meadow into something very special. Meg wouldn't say it out loud because it would sound silly, but it looked like a fairy circle to her, a magical place made out of lights and trees and carpeted in wildflowers and silvery grass. She couldn't wait to see it lit up tomorrow night, but for now all the solar cells were tested and then turned off. They would have to wait to see how it looked tomorrow afternoon.

Cars started arriving shortly after noon. The drive of choice of Joshua's many friends and relations seemed to be beat-up pickups, and soon the place looked like it was half fairy circle and half used car lot. There was a lot of laughing and unpacking, and the woods around the cabin sprouted tents like overgrown wildflowers. Catherine was able to convince most of the guests to drive down to the valley and park there to ease the crowding. And besides, now was the perfect time to head down the road: the tug-of-war was scheduled for three o'clock.

Joshua's Monster was there to carry many of them, a half-destroyed, half-restored old Hummer he and Uncle Jacob loved to work on. Everyone insisted Leah ride shotgun, leaving Meg and a herd of Joshua's high school buddies to find a place in the back where they could hold on. Gage was late getting to the Hummer, and there was a lot of good-natured groaning as everyone had to readjust to make room. As he climbed up, stepping on someone's leg by accident, she noticed he still had his jeans and work boots on. "You sure you want to swim in those?" she asked, pointing.

Gage looked down at his shoes, looked down at her, and grinned. Then he stepped on a few fingers as he altered his route and plopped down beside her, right on top of her messenger bag. She yanked it out from under him and hoped nothing in it was broken. "I won't be swimming," he said.

"You're not going to be in the tug-of-war?"

"I am. But I'm going to be on the winning side."

"Aha!" Joshua called from the front. "You must be on my side, then." The engine roared and smoke belched out in a cloud all around them. She waved it away, thinking a swim sounded good, just to wash the fumes off.

Meg noticed Leah had a stiff smile on her face. Her wedding was filled with Joshua's friends, family, and allies. They must have seemed kind enough, but their ties went deep with Joshua. Most of the people here had probably spent as much time at this cabin, at one time or another, as Meg had. It had been in the Parks family for generations, and it was everyone's favorite gathering place. Something about Catherine attracted stray kids like some people attracted mosquitoes.

Meg needed to even the score for Leah.

"I see," she said to Gage. "Yours is the hairy, smelly side. You guys can all buddy up with Joshua, chest butt each other, high five, grunt, whatever. I'm sure none of you would want to be on the bride's side. You might get girl germs."

One of the young men raised his hand and almost got knocked off the Hummer as it lurched forward. Once he righted himself he said, "I'll be on the girls' team. I'm secure in my masculinity. I'll be even more secure surrounded by women."

There was a chorus of responses that seemed to run about fifty-fifty for each side. The conversation degenerated from there as everyone debated whether it was strategically better to be on the smelly team because of the intimidation factor or if being on the smelly team could deplete your oxygen supply and make it harder to win. She tried to catch a glimpse of Leah, but Gage was blocking her view.

Please, God, let Leah know we want her to be part of the family, she prayed. For the first time Meg wished that Leah's real maid of honor Brie wasn't sick, not just because she would be free of the dress and all the rest, but because she didn't want Leah to feel alone. Leaving her home to move to Montana was a big enough sacrifice as it was.

She felt an almost itchy feeling. She was pretty sure Gage was staring at her again. He even sat taller than her, so there was no way to sneak a peek to be sure unless she was willing to look straight up into his face. She wasn't. His voice sounded very close when he said, "I'll make a bet with you."

"I don't make bets."

"If I stay dry, you tell Josh and Leah about Mouse. If I get dunked, I'll be your personal valet for the rest of the day."

Meg finally turned her face up to his. He was uncomfortably close, but he didn't seem uncomfortable at all. "I don't need a valet."

"You might like it. I'm pretty handy."

Meg glanced down at her flattened messenger bag. "I noticed that."

He gave her that same grin, that invitation to trouble. She had absolutely no idea what he was thinking, but it didn't bode well for her.

There was a large dirt parking lot just down the road, a remnant of the old cattle loading chute and corrals. The wood structures there were still standing. In fact, they were still straight. Her grandparents and great-grandparents had built the corrals, and the cabin, to last. Most of the vehicles followed Joshua down to the lot, and soon everyone was gathered. Even Meg's aunts and uncles were there, and she was grateful her uncle Jacob was wearing jeans and not shorts. She had seen him in shorts once before and had almost been blinded by his sun-starved legs.

Really, it was a silly sight. Everyone who knew about this particular Parks family tradition was wearing some odd combination of swimming and hiking clothes. Some were smart enough to bring gloves, and Meg wished she had. One year the tug-of-war left her with blisters and a rope burn where she had stubbornly wrapped the end of the rope around her wrist.

They walked a half mile down to where a footbridge crossed the creek below Little Canyon, a place where the creek had found a path through granite, probably along an old fault line. The creek behaved itself through most of the valley, meandering and flooding a wide basin that left easy access for cattle, but here it hit a granite barrier, and when it finally emerged from the canyon, the water pooled in a wonderful, deep swimming hole.

Wedding guests crowded the little footbridge and probably taxed its strength, but the bridge had been tested before and it was still standing. Joshua's team was on the far side of the creek. She and Leah walked to the other side, the steep side. Meg preferred it. It was better to hit water if you got pulled in than it was to land face first in the muddy slope on their side. She winced at a memory of it.

Jacob, Joshua's father, lined up at the end of the rope on the far side, with Joshua just in front of him. They'd be the last to go in if they lost. Cadence and two of Joshua's buddies offered to ferry the rest of rope across to their own side, and after a lot of flirting and splashing they managed to toss the other end up onto the rocky ledge. Catherine took hold of her end of the rope and led Leah backward away from the edge.

The trash talking was in full swing now. As the slack in the rope that hung over the swimming hole was pulled taut, everyone's competitive juices were flowing. The fall wouldn't kill you, but if you got tugged into the water about six feet below, you were guaranteed to feel it. Meg got pulled into line just ahead of Leah, and Cadence was next. A few young men jumped at the opportunity to line up with her.

It wasn't clear who was going to start the actual tug in this war, and legends were bound to be created on both sides, but it seemed to Meg like the team in front of her stumbled backward and she heard a few screams and splashes. However it had started, the war was on.

Meg grabbed hold and started pulling. She could hardly see ahead of her, but her feet were moving in the right direction. Then again, the grass was slick and she could have been spinning her wheels. She turned toward Leah, who looked fierce. Behind her Catherine, their anchor, looked peaceful. "Is that as hard as you can pull?" Cadence said to her team of admirers, and the dirt and grass really started to fly.

It was a good thing the other team had lost a few members in that first maneuver. "You guys pull like girls," someone from the other side yelled. Ahead of her, Aunt Sonya, Pastor Jeffrey's wife, yelled back, "Too bad you guys don't pull like men!"

Meg felt her feet slide and then heard a splash. The rope moved again, and she could hear the other side celebrating. "Pull!" Catherine commanded, and they dug in their heels. Soon there were a few other splashes, all on the other side of the swimming hole. But just when Meg was thinking they had a chance, the rope was jerked out of her hand. Someone had probably "bungeed"—held on to the rope all the way down. Leah landed on top of her, and ahead of her several women were unceremoniously dumped into the water.

Some of the wedding guests who were now out of the game were slowly making their way out of the swimming hole and up onto the footbridge, where they were shouting silly insults or doing ridiculously bad cheers.

At one point the other team was so busy laughing they could hardly stand, let alone pull. Leah must have seen the same thing. "Now!" Leah ordered, and they pulled with all their might. A very satisfying amount of shouting and splashing came from the other side of the swimming hole before things evened out again. All that remained between Meg and the water were two young men and Cadence. Without warning the man in front of Cadence slipped, and he fell off the ledge but refused to let go of the rope.

The rope jerked down in her hands, but Meg held on. Somehow they managed to pull two people from the other team off their side, but the last young man on the bride's team was trying to pull and lift his buddy back onto the ledge at the same time, and after a flailing somersault they both landed in the water. Cadence was suddenly facing the ledge, and on the other side of the swimming hole there were three men: Gage, the groom, and the groom's father. It did not look good.

Worst of all, Gage was up front, standing there in his jeans and T-shirt and his nice, dry boots.

Meg didn't want a valet. And she didn't want to lose, either. Cadence was giggling and shrieking all at the same time, and Meg and Catherine were pulling with all their might, but the rope was moving the wrong way.

Her foot twisted in a strange way, and a thought came to her. Not a very nice thought, but there it was.

"Ow!" she cried. She hopped onto her other leg, letting go of the rope with one hand to reach down and touch an ankle that didn't really hurt at all.

Meg wasn't the type to cry out, let alone cry wolf, and so the response on the other side was instantaneous.

All three men stopped pulling and stood straight up. Still hunched over, Meg turned to Leah, who had a worried look on her face. "On the count of three," Meg whispered. "One, two . . ." Luckily, by the time she reached three, both women had realized the deception. "Three!"

It looked to her like Gage was the only person actually pulling on the other side, and as Joshua and Jacob suddenly fought to dig in, Gage went flying. He tried to catch himself. A bad idea. He slid boots first down the first part of the slope, tried to stay on his feet, and arms and legs spinning like windmills, he went face first into the water. It was an epic moment, and the crowd went wild.

As it turned out, the two men on the other side were still better than Meg, Leah, and Aunt Catherine combined. Meg fought hard, and when the end came, she went in after uttering the war cry: "Get him, Leah!"

The jerk on the rope spun her backward and she landed hip first and cockeyed. She came up sputtering. The other two women were still on the ledge. Shocked, she treaded water over toward Joshua's side. Oh, he was in a pickle now. Was he really going to pull his fiancée and mom into the swimming hole? Or for that matter, would Jacob pull in his wife and daughter-in-law to be? The wedding guests were shouting for both teams to pull. Meg saw the agony on their faces and started to laugh. Just then there was a hard pull on her ankle and she went under again. She came up spitting water this time. She looked around and saw movement under the water. Gage.

Meg started swimming hard, but she didn't get far before he pulled her down again. She came up a third time feeling miffed and facing a grinning best man. For someone swimming in work boots he sure moved fast. "Ankle feeling better?" he asked.

She splashed him. He ducked under and popped up several feet away. "Don't you dare," she said.

"Or what?"

Desperate, she said, "You said you'd be my valet. Valets don't dunk."

He considered that as he circled her. There was no way she could swim fast enough to get away, that was clear. He hadn't planned on getting wet, but he seemed awfully comfortable in the water.

She looked up again. Joshua was holding the rope still, and the women were pulling with all their might. Finally he shook his head. "I can't do it," he said, laughing. "Why don't we just call a truce?"

Oh, the groans and shouts from the crowd. Even Gage stopped circling her long enough to register his disapproval. As Joshua was trying to quiet the crowd with outstretched hands the people in the water responded by trying to splash him.

Then two amazing things happened. First Jacob, strong and silent and steady Jacob, put one meaty hand on his son's back and shoved. Joshua fell to the water below. The crowd was unanimous in its approval, and Jacob bowed his head slightly to acknowledge it.

Then Leah, the Austin city girl whose makeup and hair were perfect, stepped away from the edge. She got a two-step running jump and flew into the air. For one perfect moment she looked like an angel, flying through the air with her arms outstretched, although angels probably don't say "Whee!" The next moment she was a wet mess like the rest of them.

On either side of the swimming hole Catherine and Jacob blew each other a kiss and dropped the rope. "The war must be over," Gage said. His voice came from right behind her. She spun around in the water to find him very close. She could see the muscles in his shoulders welling up with each slow stoke of his arms. "And no casualties. Not so much as a sprained ankle. Looks like I'm at your disposal, Mouse Girl. Next time I'll check the fine print on any contract with you, though."

Mouse Girl? Very funny. Was he ever going to let the whole book thing drop? It wasn't anything big. It wasn't exactly a best seller or a Caldecott award winner. She might have been more irritated if she didn't feel badly about faking a hurt ankle. "I'm sorry. And I won't hold you to the bet. In fact, I never really agreed to it in the first place." More of Gage's help was probably the last thing on earth that she needed, anyway. A few more people were voluntarily dunking themselves back into the swimming hole, and she swam downstream to get out of their way.

"Nope. I am a man of my word. Shall I rescue you from the water now? Arrange for transport to the bridge? Fan you dry with a pine bough?"

"Oh, you're funny."

"So I've been told." Down he went again. Anticipating being dunked made her heart race. And where was Leah, anyway? Meg spotted her, put her head down, and swam upstream with all her might. When she was getting close she realized Leah and Joshua were playing their own game, something that was half about splashing each other and half about cuddling. Meg didn't want to interrupt that. She spotted Cadence and some other young women up above on the ledge. There were several young men below her trying to get her to jump, but not trying very hard because the view was fine. Her aunts and uncles were finding perches on the edges to dry in the sunshine and watch the silliness below.

She knew many of the people here but not as well as Joshua knew them. He had lived here full time until moving to Texas for graduate school. During her visits she had spent so many hours in this swimming hole she thought the turquoise water must run through her veins. It seemed a lot colder than she remembered, though. It was the first week in June, and the waters were still high and icy from the snowmelt.

If she had a wedding, it couldn't be full of high school friends, she thought. She had gone to school so many places that it taxed her memory to remember them all. Those friendships hadn't lasted.

Gage popped up nearby and shook the water out of his hair directly into her face. "Are you lost?" he asked with a smile. "Actually, you look cold. Your lips are kind of blue. You can pull off the Goth look better than I would've thought."

Ha! But he was right; instead of getting used to the cold she just seemed to be getting colder. "Where is that transportation you were going to arrange?"

"Oh, I've got that covered. Hold on right here." He gestured to the water, and it seemed to her—could it be?—that he was pointing to his rear end.

She blinked. "Whatever you mean, I think not."

He looked embarrassed. "I didn't mean . . . I wouldn't ask . . . I meant my belt. In the back. Stop laughing at me."

She couldn't help it. She thought he might actually be blushing. Shivering, she swam one stroke closer and reached for his belt. "Why am I doing this again?"

"Transportation. Hold on," he said. He went a little out of the water, dove down, and dunked her again. But for some reason she didn't let go, and when she surfaced she was racing across the water. Gage wasn't just a good swimmer, he was faster than anyone she could ever remember swimming with. Startled, and laughing, Meg held on and tried to stay to the side, out of the way of his legs. She flew across the swimming hole. She hoped dragging her this way wouldn't make his belt slide off.

The water was shallow near the bridge, and she let go and stood up. She felt heavy, messy, and very cold. Gage stood up too, looking very fine in his wet shirt, wet jeans, and ruined cowboy boots. He shook his head and sprayed her again. "Shall I carry you to the top?"

"Absolutely not," she said with a laugh. "So I take it you've done a little swimming before?"

He nodded. "I competed in college. And if you don't mind, I think I'm going to get a little more swimming in before I get out for good." He reached down, pulled off a boot, then upended it. Water poured out, and it was so comical Meg couldn't help but laugh out loud. "I'm sorry," she said.

"I can tell." He did the same to the other boot.

"I'll put those in the sun for you," she said, reaching for the boots. "I'm not sure it's going to do much good, though."

Gage waded a couple of steps deeper and dove out into the water. He disappeared beneath the surface. She waited for a minute to see if he would surface, wondering if he might in fact have gills. But her shivering was getting worse, so she climbed the grassy slope up into the mountain sunshine.

It was so beautiful. There was hardly a breath of wind, and the sun was warm and high even this late in the afternoon. Blue lupines and bunches of showy, golden arrowleaf balsamroot blanketed the valley. The air smelled faintly of pine and the rocky, clean scent of rushing water. She often felt an ache at moments like this, knowing that the river-bottom land once belonged to her family but didn't anymore. Now it was a jumble of water rights, mining claims, grazing leases, public lands, and private inholdings owned mostly by a land company out of Pennsylvania. Its future was uncertain.

She doubted anything could make Joshua let go of the cabin and its 160 acres, though. Her many cousins would soon start families of their own. Joshua and Leah were welcoming, but they couldn't be expected to keep letting everyone come here whenever they liked. There were just too many Parks around, now.

It was Joshua's cabin, and that was just as well, because if her parents had inherited it they would have sold it in an instant to fund their latest mission. They would always have an empty bank account and a new mailing address.

Meg wondered what legacy she would leave to her children, and whether she would ever have any kids. What sort of husband would she want, and who would want her at the same time? The whole thing seemed so unlikely that she sighed and chased the thought from her mind.

Leah rose up out of the creek bed nearby, looking frozen to the bone. "That was crazy," she said. "Y'all are nuts."

"You won."

"Sort of. Oh, and you with the hurt ankle! I about fell over. When Gage went in the water, it was all I could do not to let go of the rope, I was laughing so hard. Good gracious, are those his boots?"

"Yep. I need to set them out to dry." Meg and Leah wandered near the top of the swimming hole and found a grassy, warm place to sit. Leah shook out her hair and tilted her face to the sun. "I saw you swimming with him. It looked like you were riding a dolphin," she teased.

"He was just being my valet. He bet me that he wouldn't end up in the water, and since he lost, he said he's going to be my valet all day."

Leah shook her head, eyes closed. "He's certainly a charmer." Then she leaned forward and looked into the swimming hole.

Meg did the same, and they could see Gage down below, playing keep away with a woman's towel. Most of the guys were in on it, but even when the towel changed hands there was a school of women swimming around Gage.

There was something in Leah's tone that was nagging at her. "I don't know about charming. He seems nice, but not my type. Why, is there something I should know about him?" Gage ducked below the surface, and a few of the girls started to splash and squeal as they tried to get away from him.

"I don't think so," Leah said. "I've never seen him be anything but polite, Meg. It's just that he's got a checkered past, and I knew him back then. He was, well, a friend of a friend. But Joshua thinks the world of him. Being Josh's roommate changed a lot of things for him."

That wasn't necessarily a compliment. Joshua found friends everywhere, but they weren't all the kind of person Meg would want to date. Gage had the towel again, and it was causing quite a commotion in the swimming hole.

Leah looked deep in thought. "I think he's a good friend, but I haven't thought about whether he'd be a good boyfriend now. A lot has changed in his life, Meg, but he and I are not close enough to discuss those things. If you ever did find him charming, I think it would be a good thing to ask him outright what kind of boyfriend he would be. In fact, it's a good question for any man you might want to date."

Meg laughed. "Leah, you sound just like Catherine."

"Really?" Leah's eyes were bright.

"Yes, really. You two have a lot in common. You're both easy to talk to." She thought about the cabin, breakfast, the wedding, and more. "You're both generous people, too."

Leah looked flattered. "Catherine is very generous. But you know that, spending so much time with her. Did you know she talks about you like you're her daughter? And for that matter, Josh talks about you like a sister."

Meg let that soak in like the sunlight, and it felt just as warm. "They always made me feel at home."

"I thought you liked being on the move. You do live out of a camper most of the time."

For some reason, Leah's words troubled her. "I don't have much choice. I go wherever the jobs are. Next week it's a community center in a small town north of here. They want a 'Say No to Drugs' mural in the gym. I'm supposed to do part of it and help the kids do the rest."

"I know you also do a lot of clipart for the Internet, and you can do that just about anywhere. It's too bad there isn't something else you could do so you wouldn't have to be on the move all the time."

Something like write? Meg wanted that. She wanted it so badly that every time she sat down to work on another storybook she felt paralyzed with fear. How much work could a muralist get? She was pretty sure she'd broken a record, at least in the state. But no one considered her bright, whimsical designs high art. The end of her current lifestyle was looming, though, lurking in the rusted Jeep hitch, the leaky water tank of her camper, and the calls that weren't coming as fast as they once had. She was three years from thirty with an associate's degree and hardly any skills that could get her a real job.

The worry and uncertainty of her parents' life was exactly what she had wanted to avoid. She had worked nearly every day for the last decade, and yet here she was . . . headed for the same place. And without the good reasons her parents always had.

She tilted her face toward the light. She needed a little more sunshine. "Can you keep a secret?"

"Not from Joshua."

That made Meg smile. "I'm glad he found you, Leah. No, I wouldn't expect you to keep it from him, but I hope you'll give me a chance to tell him myself sometime in the next few months."

"Well, if it isn't something like a serious illness or an upcoming marriage, I suppose I can hold off telling him for a little bit."

"It's not. It's stupid, really. I never told anyone, but I wrote and illustrated a children's book. It was kind of a fluke. I made a booklet to go with one of my murals at a school, and a teacher there pulled some strings with an agent friend of hers. The next thing I knew it was published. Sales were slow at first, and I didn't expect anything different, but now for some reason they're picking up. The publisher wants to do another book and make it a big media blitz."

Leah looked happy and, surprisingly, not shocked. "That's wonderful, Meg! Why on earth would you want to keep that secret?"

Meg tried to put it in words, but each time she tried

it got stuck in her throat and she didn't want to have to spit it out.

"You're worried it's all going to fall apart, aren't you?" Leah said.

Meg nodded with relief. "That's a big part of it."

"Never mind that. Josh is going to be so happy for you. And Catherine. Except she's going to kill you for not telling her."

"Don't I know it."

Right on cue, Joshua climbed out onto the grassy shore and called out, "Are you two talking about me?"

Josh hugged Leah like he hadn't seen her in hours. "I'm starving," he said. "It must be time to barbecue. Uh-oh, are those Gage's boots?"

There was a photo session with the drenched and dirty crew back at the parking lot. Meg tried to bury herself in the middle of the crowd. Gage stood behind her, his soggy boots back on. He and Josh's brother, Caleb, put the groom up on their shoulders, and Josh managed to stay up there just long enough for a few pictures before he crashed down into the waiting arms of his bride and wedding guests.

It was an even tighter fit in the Monster because many of the guests left their cars behind to make room for the wedding. Meg kept her messenger bag tucked into her lap and sat near the edge of the vehicle as it started back up toward the cabin.

The dinner barbecue was supposed to be the responsibility of the men of the wedding party, Joshua, Gage, and Caleb. When she overheard Leah say she wanted to take an hour off for a nap, Meg saw her chance to have a few moments to herself and asked Josh to drop her off at the old logging road on the way. When he stopped, she slipped off the side, said a quick good-bye to Leah, and then backed away.

Gage started to stand up as if he were going to follow her. He was taking this valet thing far too seriously, she realized. She waved, the Monster lurched, and Gage sat back down hard. She turned and walked down the grassy roadway as other cars passed by behind her. It felt like she had her own private retreat, and she relished this moment of rest. Sure, she could use a shower, but it could wait a few minutes for her to drink a glass of water and maybe lie down for a bit.

She woke up feeling light-headed, disoriented, and anxious. How long had she been asleep? Meg checked her watch. She hoped she hadn't missed out on any maid of honor duties. Her dream was still buzzing around in her head, something about the stream and a flash flood, and Gage swimming hard. He'd turned into a dolphin, hadn't he, and stranded her in the middle of the ocean? Meg shook her head. Weird, very weird. Here she'd finally gotten away from him and he had found a way to get into her dreams.

She sat on the edge of the bed. Her sketchbook was still on the table, open to a blank page. The publisher wanted a proposal by the end of next week, and Whitehall School District wanted her to come for an interview on Monday. If she took that job, they wanted the mural done the second week of school, along with presentations to the school assembly.

And that conflicted with the book signing her publisher wanted her to do that week. The thought of a book signing filled her with dread. There would be adults there—even worse, there would be parents there, scrutinizing her work. Would they sense God's presence in her story? Would they be offended, one way or another? Would there be enough colors of fur among the animals? Would they take offense to a bad word like "bottom"? Ugh. Talking to kids was fun. Talking to adults was a minefield.

She hooked the hose to the faucet, opened the window, and fed the hose through. It only took a moment to put the shower head on it and hang the shower tent on the outside of the camper, since she had installed a folding hook. She did a careful check of the woods: no voices or signs of movement, as she expected.

Back inside the camper, she slipped out of her damp clothes, put on a towel and a pair of flip-flops, and grabbed her shampoo. There was so much privacy in the woods here she didn't feel the need to keep her bathing suit on. The very last thing was to turn on the hot and cold water to just the right combination. She set the faucet and then hurried outside so she didn't waste any precious water.

She hung the towel on its own special hook and ducked in under the drizzle of water—yikes! Still cold! She backed off and shampooed her hair until the water warmed up. The shampoo made a fine soap, too, and in a flash the mud and grass from the creek, and possibly the Monster's exhaust fumes, were gone. She rinsed with a sigh. It felt so good.

She grabbed her towel, wrapped herself in it, and dashed out of the shower stall to turn off the water. She only made it three steps before she heard a gasp and looked up to see Gage standing in front of her holding something big and green. She screamed.

He looked absolutely shocked. Her mind was in a whirl. She'd run out of water if she didn't turn it off soon, and she wasn't entirely sure what her crumpled towel was covering. Worse, rearranging it could be perilous. She had to get to the door on the other side of the camper, but she couldn't turn her back because she was sure her rear towel coverage was not sufficient. How could she back over the hitch without showing too much? And was that a car motor she heard behind her?

Gage looked down. "I actually wanted to give you—"

Frustrated and embarrassed, she cut him off with a loud, "Go!" She backed around the corner, around the hitch, and through the door, half expecting him to come after her. He started to say something else, but she was so flustered she added, "Just go away!" for extra protection. In a second the door was closed and latched, the water was off, and Meg stood dripping on the mud she'd tracked in. She usually left her flip-flops outside. She also usually wasn't on a postshower run from tall Texans.

She couldn't hear him. She waited for a knock on the door, but it didn't come. She was afraid to look out the window at first, but finally she did and she saw no sign of him. Gage was gone. She breathed a sigh of relief.

What on earth was he up to? Could he have made an honest mistake? Well, there was nothing honest about sneaking up on a girl in the shower. She wondered briefly about her conversation with Leah. Just exactly what checkered past did Gage have? She shook her head. It was none of her business, not that Leah would tell her, anyway. More importantly, she didn't care. He had left, she was fine, and sometime after the wedding he would be flying back to Texas. She had never seen him before, so she was pretty certain she'd never have to see him again.

Meg put on "comfort clothes": her favorite jeans, her favorite cute-but-soft shirt, and her favorite boots. Ugh, Gage's boots. Would they have survived if she hadn't feigned an injury? That wasn't fair at all. She regretted doing it. And at the same time, she didn't. She turned on the camper's master switch just long enough to use the travel dryer to dry her hair a little, and then she put on a little makeup. Not too much, just a little went a long way with her fair skin and gray eyes. Bright colors—colors like Kelly green—made her look pale or sick. Meg laughed out loud and shook her head. Other than the dress, she was beginning to look forward to being Leah's maid of honor.

She reached for her messenger bag and realized she had never checked it for damage. A tube of sun block had been squished open, but the mess could have been worse. She wiped it out. It was an easier thing to fix than Gage's boots. She put a nice fleece jacket inside the bag. It was still hot outside now, but it never stayed that way in the mountains.

Meg left the camper and, for the first time all weekend, locked the door. She wandered down the logging road slowly, listening to the birds. She watched a chickadee shell a seed on the branch of a pine tree and wished she had time to stop and sketch, but she didn't. Leah would either be awake or have given up on napping by now. Meg wanted to help out any way she could.

She was so engrossed in the bird and he was sitting so still that Meg didn't see Gage seated on a rock at the end of the logging road. He looked mad. She didn't think he had anything to be mad about. He glanced up at her and let out a big sigh. "I'm sorry," he said. He didn't sound sorry, he sounded irritated.

She took a few cautious steps forward. He still had that big green thing in his arms, and she wanted to get a closer look. "You have a towel," she said.

"Yeah. Ironic, isn't it?"

"You were bringing me a towel."

"I thought it would be funny. I thought it was just the sort of thing a valet would do. I didn't actually think you'd be taking a shower, outside, naked. At least I think you were, not that I . . . what were you thinking?"

"I wasn't thinking that I'd be running into a Peeping Texan."

He grumbled and rubbed his palm against his forehead. "Yeah. Here, you want this?" He stood up and held the towel out to her. She recognized it from the large stash of towels at the cabin. Something darker green and shiny was sitting on top of it, though. He noticed her looking, and snatched it off and shoved it into his back pocket. "I ate the mint."

He'd brought her a towel and a mint. She didn't know whether to be amused or freaked out. To give herself a little time to decide, she took the towel back to the camper. And she locked it again. Then she came back to find Gage still waiting, and still looking cranky. He looked that way as he took the messenger bag from her and slung it over his own shoulder and the whole time they walked up the long driveway.

When they came in sight of the cabin and the guests gathered in camp chairs in the meadow, he handed the bag back to her. "Thank you," he said. She didn't know what he was thanking her for, but before she could ask, Joshua was waving a spatula and calling him over.

"It's about time!" Josh was yelling at him.

Meg spotted a few friends she had not seen earlier and went over to catch up. A few minutes later she caught sight of Leah on the deck, and she headed that way, even though it meant being near Gage. He was still with the other men at the new grill. Leah came over and gave her a hug. "Did you get some rest?"

Meg nodded. "Did you?"

"I did! Josh found some earplugs for shooting and I put those in and slept like a baby. I'm so glad we got most of the decorations done. Catherine has tomorrow's reception dinner covered, and Josh and Caleb have dinner covered. Well, sort of; they've been arguing about the right way to grill, of course. And I see Gage went down to visit you again."

"He is my valet."

"Mm hmm," Leah said, adding a little Texas drawl to the sound. "And I suppose a man deciding to become your valet happens to you all the time."

"Oh, yes, of course. Doesn't it happen to everyone?"

"Only once for me, and now I'm marrying him."

Meg gave her a warning glance. "Don't even let it cross your mind, Leah."

"I'm not thinking anything except what a beautiful day it is."

They were soon handing out paper plates full of potato salad, hamburgers, and brats. Cadence gathered orders like a pro, Leah and Meg assembled the plates to be delivered, and Josh, Caleb, and Gage argued about when to flip and what constituted done. Up on the edge of the deck as they were, they looked like a comedy routine on a stage. As far as Meg could tell, Joshua told everyone what to do, Caleb told him he was wrong, and Gage did it his own way anyway. Leah and Meg had to stop twice they were laughing so hard.

Eventually everybody but the servers had a plate, and Joshua made up one for Leah, explaining that he put the sweet relish on her brat even though he thought it was awful and she really should try the dill. When Meg reached for a plate for herself, Gage grabbed it out of her hand. "Dog or burger?"

"Burger, please."

"And how do you like it done?"

"Anything but burned."

Gage glared at the burner. "I think we may be out of those. How about singed?"

Meg peeked at the grill. He wasn't exaggerating. "That would be great."

He got her ketchup, pickles, no relish of any kind, and potato salad order ready for her. She reached for her plate again, and again he pulled it away. "Where would you like to sit?"

Leah, who was finding the whole routine amusing, patted the seat next to her. On her other side, Joshua was busy poking his brother in the shoulder for some reason. Meg sat down next to Leah, and Gage set the plate down in front of her and disappeared into the crowd. Meg closed her eyes and sighed. The man was relentless. When she opened her eyes, it occurred to her that she didn't have any silverware or anything to drink, but before she could get up again, he reappeared to drape a paper napkin across her lap. Another paper napkin was over his left arm, and he was holding a small bottle of citrus soda over the towel like a fine wine. "Will the green do, or would you like the brown vintage?"

"Green, please."

Gage opened it and handed her the cap. "Would you like to sniff the cork?"

She gave him the stink eye and Leah giggled. As he went to pour out the soda he realized she didn't have a cup. It took him three more trips to assemble a cup and fork and to get his own plate. Then Gage pulled a chair closer to her and sat down, knocking her elbow and dropping some potato salad into her lap. He didn't even notice. Luckily the napkin was there to catch it.

Joshua and Caleb were now loudly playing some sort of game that involved flicking each other with a finger. It looked painful. Leah gestured to them and asked Meg, "Are they always like this?"

Meg nodded. "Don't ask me why."

"Maybe their love language is flicking," Gage said.

Leah's eyebrows raised. "Love language? Are you reading marriage books?"

"Nope. Parenting books." He let that comment hang in the air for a while. Leah and Meg were both silent, waiting for another shoe to drop.

"My sister made me read a couple parts of a book," Gage continued. "She was trying to figure out which love language my nephew had. I said he was five and the only love language she needed to know about was the hold-him-down-and-tickle-him language. It's a pretty good sign if, when you stop, the kid starts screaming for more. I figure when he gets a little older he'll speak the driving-too-fast-on-the-four-wheeler language. I'm fluent in that one, too."

"Boys," someone said firmly, and years of experience brought Meg to attention. It worked on Joshua and Caleb, too, and the flicking stopped. Catherine sat down at the table with them, glowered at her sons, and then smiled sweetly at Leah. "How are you holding up?"

"I'm excited," she said, and she looked that way, Meg thought.

"We're taking a lot of people down to the house tonight, just to let you know. Hopefully the rest of them won't keep you up all night."

"Sonya's dance lesson should tire them out!"

So Sonya was in charge of today's mysterious dance lesson. That didn't reveal anything at all, since Sonya liked all kinds of social dancing. Meg asked for more details, but Catherine and Leah weren't talking. "They don't want us to know so we don't make a break for it," Joshua said. "And don't ask me, I'm sworn to secrecy."

"It had better not be clogging," Caleb offered. "Aunt Sonya just about made me crazy the Christmas she took up clogging."

Meg gave Catherine a pleading look. "Please tell me it isn't," she said.

Catherine smiled. "I'm not telling."

All the men at the table moaned. "That would be the worst thing ever," Caleb said.

"No," Gage said. "Line dancing would be worse." That brought an even louder moan.

"I like line dancing," Leah said. "What's wrong with that?"

"Line dancing is for girls," Caleb informed her. "Men don't line dance."

"I've seen cowboys line dance."

"Then it must have been in Texas, because no self-respecting Montana cowboy would ever be caught line dancing."

"Hey, now." Gage held his palm up in an attempt to stop Caleb.

Caleb was undaunted, and he gave Gage a scrutinizing look. "Well, have you ever line danced?"

There was a brief, deep silence at the table, until Meg and Leah started laughing. Caleb waved an accusing fork at Gage, and Joshua smacked his forehead with the palm of his hand. "I can't believe you're my best man."

"That's where all the women were." As soon as the words were out of Gage's mouth, he turned to Meg and insisted, "That was a long time ago." She could have sworn his face was turning red. Was it over the line dancing or chasing women?

Catherine interrupted the commotion. "Well, we all know that Texas is where the real cowboys are."

No, Aunt Catherine wouldn't do that to her, would she? Some stories were meant to fade into obscurity, and hers was definitely one of them. She could feel her own face starting to get hot.

Joshua's eyes grew wide and he started laughing, which was not pretty because he had just taken another bite of hamburger. "I almost forgot about that!" he said. Everyone else at the table looked confused.

Meg shot Catherine a pleading look, but she knew it wouldn't do any good. "One summer Meg said she wanted us to all go to Texas so she could meet a real cowboy."

That started a cacophony of laughter and a flurry of fork waving. "I was ten," Meg said, but she was pretty sure no one heard her. She shook her head and laughed at herself. She could barely remember her reasoning at the time, but it had something to do with a movie she'd seen. Since she was a member of a family with cattle ranching in their blood, the story might live forever.

Gage turned to her with his trouble-causing grin. The second things were quiet enough, he said, "Did you ever make it to Texas?"

She shook her head, feeling like she was being set up for a punch line.

"Then that pretty much makes me your dream come true."

More groans and laughter followed, during which Meg said, "You line dance and haven't got any cowboy boots. You can't possibly be a real cowboy."

His grin never wavered. "Darlin', I've got another pair, and I'll go clogging in them if I have to."

Soon after dinner Sonya took over. As a pastor's wife, she had perfected the art of gently coercing people, and her skills were on display this evening. The wedding invitation had encouraged all musicians to bring their instruments. Now Sonya sent the musicians off in search of one, and in record time she had them playing a simple folk tune with just four chords. It was lively and sounded vaguely Celtic to Meg. Things didn't seem to be going well for the anticlogging crowd.

It was the most beautiful time of day. The sun was low in the west but not yet setting, the scattered wildflowers were still blooming, but there was a hint of a cooler breeze. It smelled of new, growing things. Things down on the flats were heating up, but June in the mountains of Montana was still springtime.

Soon everyone else was summoned to the "dance floor," the part of the meadow that would be the aisle of a wedding chapel the next day. Sonya told everyone to find a partner, and Gage instantly took Meg by the elbow. "This is part of my valet duty," he assured her. Sonya had everyone line up across from their partner, women and girls on one side and men and boys on the other. It was a motley bunch of dancers, with kids and grandparents and complete strangers paired up. Those who tried to hide were lured in by whatever charm, or threats, Sonya felt it necessary to use.

She had every other couple switch places to mix the boys and girls. Now Meg was standing across from Gage and between Caleb and Joshua. "This looks like square dancing," Joshua said.

"This isn't a square, it's a rectangle," Caleb corrected his brother.

Sonya informed everyone that they would be doing four, count them, four moves, and anyone on earth could learn that many. She also said they'd better learn them because they would do them over and over again for the next twenty minutes.

She called it contra dancing. For the first move, everyone stepped forward, passed in back of their partner, and backed up to where they were. It took a ridiculously long time for everyone to get it right, which made them all laugh. For the second move, the women turned to the man on their left and they both got into a ballroom dancing position and turned around one and a half times. There were two more moves, and when all the moves were completed in order, Meg and Gage had moved one position toward the right, giving them a new set of neighbors to dance with.

Sonya kept everyone going until all she had to do was call out the name of the move, and then she had the makeshift band begin to play. "Slowly," she suggested. "At least at first." The music started, sounding not much better than an orchestra tuning up. And the crowd of dancers were a disaster. But Sonya kept cheerfully calling out the steps and words of encouragement.

Just when it all seemed hopeless, something shifted. The band found its rhythm and so did the dancers. Any time Meg forgot the next move, there was a partner there who remembered it, and the reverse was true as well. For each round she do-si-doed and swung once with Gage and then with whoever was to her left. When they hit the end of the long line, they switched places and came back the other way.

Because of the way contra dancing worked, Meg ended up dancing with every single man and boy in the long line, and she laughed her way through every bit of it. Gage was smiling and gracious to every dance partner and was pretty smooth on his tennis-shoed feet. When they made it through the whole line, Sonya encouraged the band to speed it up, and they danced faster and faster until it all fell apart in a foot-stomping, hilarious mess. The band took a well-deserved bow, and a few of the dancers and musicians offered to switch places.

There was hardly enough time to get some water before Sonya was teaching the band another simple song. This time almost everyone came back to make happy fools of themselves again, no coercion needed. Sonya added two new moves to their repertoire and arranged them in a new combination, and as complicated as it seemed at first, Meg got to a point where Sonya calling the next move seemed to go straight from her ear to her feet without her having to think about it.

It was evening, but during summer in Montana the sun lingers into the night. The cooler air soothed the dancers, who had worked up a sweat. It was a hardcore and determined crew of newborn contra dancers that stayed for a third and then a fourth song—and demanded something more complex. Sonya's voice was getting hoarse but not quieter. She led them through new moves and patterns with enthusiasm. Meg wished she could have seen the dancers from above, as they must have looked like flowers unfolding and shifting across the meadow.

Meg was beginning to like the moment in each cycle when she came back to Gage's arms. He was tall, that was certain. But he had a way of holding her that was firm and steady. They could spin like crazy across the dirt and grass, but his arms were like the eye of the storm. For someone who seemed to break things a lot, there was nothing but grace in his dancing.

And while it seemed at first that she had to lean back

to look him in the face, she found that up close she didn't notice very much other than his amber eyes and the dark streaks of sweat at his temples that did little to tame his wavy hair. And always, every moment he held her, the grin. She couldn't help but smile back.

Then he would gently lead her into the next move, charm his next dance partner, and be there to pull Meg into the dance again.

When the song was over, the musicians nursed sore fingers, the dancers were worn out, and Sonya sounded like a frog. Meg teased Caleb about line dancing, since they had in fact been in a line, and Caleb said that if you got to hold a girl it didn't count. That sounded a lot like Gage's reasoning to her and she would have teased him, but Meg let the conversation drop because Caleb seemed to have his eye on one of Joshua's friends. As she expected, he scurried over to where the girl was standing.

A plastic glass of water appeared in front of her. "Here you go, Mouse Girl. Turns out you can dance as well as you write."

She wrinkled her nose at him. "Thanks for the water." She looked through the crowd until she spotted Leah, who was sitting with Joshua.

"Leah's fine," Gage said, without looking behind him to see what she was looking at. "You've been looking like a nervous mother hen."

"I have not!" Had she? Meg hoped Leah hadn't noticed.

"So how does she look to you?"

Leah was smiling, and Joshua reached up gently to lift a strand of hair from her face. "Happy," Meg said. "Josh, too."

"I think your work here is done," Gage said with a

smile. "All that's left to do is walk down the aisle without tripping."

She laughed. "Oh, sure, plant that idea in my mind. And it's not as easy as it seems!"

"From what I've seen, you could dance down it very well."

"Wouldn't that be classy? No, I'll walk down, high heels and all. The skirt on that dress is so skinny I'll have to take itty bitty steps, so there's no chance I'll be going too fast, either. And I may have to arrange the bride's train or swat a bee. Or fan Leah's face if she faints. Or bounce the hordes of rejected women who will be weeping in the back as Joshua is taken off the market. It's a very complicated job, being the maid of honor."

"Yes, but I'm the one who has to catch Joshua if he faints. I also have to pin the flower to my lapel without bleeding on anything, and I have to entertain—"

"The hordes of rejected women?"

He shook his head firmly. "I'll leave that to a younger and much more foolish man." He was lost in thought for a moment before adding, "I was going to say, entertain the maid of honor." He gestured to the deck, where they turned two chairs toward the meadow and sat down. Off to their right, near the edge of the meadow, Joshua and Caleb now seemed to be arguing about the fire pit while Uncle Jacob ignored them both and poured on some gasoline.

"You won't have to be entertaining the maid of honor, your job as valet will be finished."

"No. It's in the job description; I looked it up at the Montana Wedding Job Services website. It specifically says I have to walk the maid of honor back down the aisle and keep her from either tripping or dancing too much. I have to dance my first dance with her, and just to make sure I did it right, at least the next six or seven dances, until she gets used to taking tiny little steps in her very snazzy, very green dress. That's unless they play the Chicken Dance, because then you'll have to fend for yourself. I am an expert, and no one can defeat me."

"I bet Aunt Sonya could give you a run for your money."

"Bring it on, Aunt Sonya."

Whoosh. Meg felt the percussion of the gasoline fireball as the fire was lit fifteen yards away. A column of fire rose, turned to a ball of black smoke, and drifted up into the dark blue sky. Jacob nodded once at his handiwork, apparently pleased. Meg couldn't be sure from here, but he seemed to still have his eyebrows. Gage applauded, and a smattering of other people applauded as well.

Meg was thinking about what Gage had said. She was also thinking about what Leah had said about his having a checkered past, and if she were to guess, that past had a lot to do with women. She decided she should let it drop, that there was no reason to get involved, but then the words slipped out of her mouth. "I'm glad to hear you're not young and foolish. Although you're not exactly old. You have to be about my age, and I'm not quite sure I can claim to be completely grown up."

He gave her an appraising look. That look said he knew exactly what she was really asking about—the hordes of women. "Well, when I started college I was pretty normal, not too smart, not too dumb. Then instead of growing up, I just got stupid. About the time I moved in with Joshua I started growing up again, and I've had a lot of catching up to do. I'm not wise, but I'm not going to be foolish anymore. At least in some areas of my life." He put his feet up on the railing and let those words hang in the air for a while. Then he added, "I'll give you some of the gory details someday. For now, let's just say that I may be a slow learner, but I'm a determined one."

Someday. Not likely, she realized, and besides, it wasn't any of her business. He would be heading back to Texas soon. "When do you fly out?"

"Sunday evening, a red-eye. I have to get back and move out of Joshua's and my place by Tuesday night. The new tenants move in a few days after. Since I found out my roommate was going to ditch me for a bride, I've been thinking a lot about where I want to move."

"Did you decide?" She told herself that she was just being polite, but there she was, being absolutely ridiculous and wishing he was about to tell her he was moving to Montana.

"I've been looking all over, but I think I'll probably end up moving nearer to my hometown. That's where my parents are, and my sister and her family. If I could be within a few hours' drive of my nephew, that would be the best thing ever."

She was going to ask more, but the sound of an engine caught her attention. She turned to see a familiar car coming up the drive. It was Catherine's Expedition, but there was no reason for her to be back so soon.

"I thought Catherine just left," Gage said. He put his feet down and leaned forward.

"She did, she went home to finish cooking the reception food before everyone invaded her home . . . and her showers." She glanced at Gage. For the first time that she had seen, he looked worried, and it gave her a bad feeling.

Joshua started walking over to the driver's side window, but Leah stayed by the bonfire, peering at him while she held a hand up to block the light from the headlights. As he approached, the passenger door opened and out bounded a tall woman. She ran forward into the beam of the lights and Leah opened her arms for the hug she got, one that nearly knocked her over.

The woman was wearing over-the-knee boots, skinny cream-colored jeans, and a leather trench coat with a belt that showed off her slim figure. Above that was a flood of shining red waves of hair. She had a stylish green scarf on and sunglasses on her head, although the sun had set. In the middle of the creek-washed, sweaty, smoky crowd in the meadow, she looked like a supermodel.

"Brie," Gage said, but Meg had already guessed that.

I bet Brie looks great in Kelly green, she thought. And although she knew she should feel happy for Leah and relieved for herself, instead she felt a sad, sinking feeling that she couldn't quite explain.

She talked herself out of that. It was wonderful that Leah's friend was here for her important day. Brie certainly looked healthy enough, and she had run faster in her high-heeled boots than Meg probably could in tennis shoes. "Looks like I'm out of a job," she joked to Gage, but when she turned back to him she saw him frowning, the knuckles of one fist pressed to his lips. He didn't seem to hear her.

Meg stepped around him to go introduce herself, but Leah and Brie were already headed toward the cabin. Behind them Meg caught sight of Joshua taking two suitcases and a purse out of the Expedition. Leah threw Meg a distraught expression as she approached, and she touched her hand to her heart. The last thing Meg wanted was for Leah to feel badly about kicking her out of the maid of honor job. She never wanted it anyway, so what did it matter? She winked at Leah. "You must be Brie," Meg said. "I'm so glad you made it! I know Leah was hoping you could."

It wasn't too dark to see the big, movie-star smile Brie gave her as she stepped up onto the deck. Meg had to look up at her. "Hi! And you are?"

"My name is Meg. I was going to be the backup maid of honor, but luckily you're feeling better now."

"Yes, it was awful. But I bounce back pretty fast." She suddenly looked over Meg's shoulder, and her eyes narrowed. "Well, if it isn't the best man. I guess you finally found a way to meet up with me again after all."

Meg glanced at Gage, who was standing behind her. His face was blank in the dim light.

"Well then! Shall we get you settled?" Joshua said, and he nudged them all forward, arms full of suitcases. Meg backed up and away from the wedding party. She stared at the faded wood of the porch, blue in the evening light.

"There's no electricity?" she heard Brie say over lower conversation. She saw a dim light through the window and knew someone was lighting the lanterns. Well, I'm off the hook, she thought. But her head felt like it was on fire. She was thinking all sorts of things, and none of them had to do with her cousin's wedding.

Leah came back out on the deck, arms outstretched. "I feel awful," she said, and her tone of voice proved it.

"Well, don't. I got to do all the fun stuff—decorate, hang out with you, and eat French toast. Leah, the fact is, I love you, and I'm really glad you're going to be a Parks. I'll be standing up for you whether I'm up front or in the back."

Leah gave her a big hug and didn't let go for a while. When she pulled back Meg spotted the sparkle of tears in Leah's eyes. "Thanks for making me feel so welcome, Meg."

Meg felt her own eyes well up, and she brushed her tears with her sleeve. "Oh, cut it out. I'm supposed to be saving all my sobbing for tomorrow."

"Leah? Which is my room?" Brie was calling. Meg backed away and Leah headed for the door. As she opened it, Gage was coming out. "Bunk beds?" said Brie's laughing voice from inside. Meg smiled, waved at both Gage and Leah, and headed for the bonfire.

But Gage ran after her. She could hear his loud steps on the deck. He touched her shoulder and she turned around, but all she could think was that she really didn't want to find out what all the tension between him and Brie was about. "I just wanted to say thanks for the dance," he said.

"You're welcome."

She was looking for a polite way out, but he seemed determined to say something else. Her Uncle Jeffrey's voice saved her. "There you are, Gage! I am so sorry it's taken me this long, I was caught up with finalizing a detail or two on the ceremony, and then the dinner, and then . . ." He looked at Meg and back at Gage again. "Do you have time to talk now, or am I interrupting something?"

"Not at all," Meg said. She gave her pastor uncle a kiss on the cheek, waved cheerfully at Gage again, and took off across the little meadow.

There was something reassuring about the smell of wood smoke. It reminded her of the end of long days of work or play, the moment when the only thing left to do is go to sleep. It felt warm and bright and lovely, but after about three minutes, she was done. Leah was fine, Joshua was fine, and soon everyone would be heading toward their tents or to Catherine and Jacob's house to sleep. It was time for her to get some rest. She had cobwebs to clear.

As she started down the dark road, she glanced back up toward the cabin. No one was following her. The day was over, and her own personal valet had moved on to another job. Part of her mind, the tricky part in the back, was imagining hearing footsteps coming up behind her and a hand on her elbow. It would be like Gage to insist on walking her down to the camper, wouldn't it?

She slipped on some loose gravel on the steep drive. It was the only sound except for the murmur of laughter above her.

He had something more important to do, now. She tried to stop listening for footsteps that weren't coming. It was a waste of time and made her head hurt. Not only did he have a new maid of honor to look after, but it was clear that they knew each other. There was no mistaking the familiarity in Brie's expression or the tension in his when she arrived. It was as if he had been caught doing something wrong.

All he had been doing was talking to Meg. Maybe even flirting, if she could remember what that was like. Maybe he was flirting with one girl when he already had made promises to another. Meg slipped on another steep spot and sighed. She was too close to the camper to bother pulling the flashlight out of her bag now.

Had he been flirting? For heaven's sake, had she? How embarrassing. She couldn't help but smile when she was talking with him, or worse, dancing with him. Her face felt funny from all the smiling she'd been doing. She rubbed at her cheek—that's what the world needed, cheek workouts. She could imagine opening a chain of stores where eager clients stood in front of a mirror and a perky girl in spandex told jokes.

Okay, now she was just getting silly. She tried to open the door and was surprised to find it locked. Oh yeah, she had locked Gage out this morning. Funny how your opinion of someone could change—or change back—in such a short time. She unlocked the door and went into her dark camper, closed the door behind her, and stood still. It was very, very quiet. All traces of the sun, the laughter, and color were gone. Instead of turning on the light, Meg sat down on her bed. She didn't feel like reading, she still had nothing to write, and she didn't have to do anything special and wedding-like with her hair anymore.

How long had it been since a man made her smile like that? It didn't matter. Like just about all new friendship she made these days, someone would be leaving soon. Usually it was her, going from job to job. She liked that better than having people, even strange people who might already have girlfriends, leave her. She dragged herself through her bedtime routine in the dark, crawled into bed, and let her tired body drag her racing mind deep into sleep.

Saturday

Bam bam bam! Meg jolted awake, but she couldn't make sense of what she was hearing or where she was. It was barely light. Her first coherent thought was that it was Gage and she didn't have any coffee ready yet. "Margaret! Are you in there?"

She got up, pulled a blanket around her shoulders, and opened the door of the camper. "Mom! Dad! Hi . . . what time is it?" Hugs were exchanged all around. The cold morning air seeped in, and she heard her little propane heater kick on. "Come in!"

Her father's blond hair had more gray, but other than that, he looked just the same. Gray eyes like his brothers and so many of the Parks clan, and a face that seemed always to be faintly smiling. Her mother had put on a couple pounds, as she usually did between missions, and she looked cute that way. Meg didn't like it when she got stringy and tired looking. No doubt Catherine had been working hard to fill her out. Her mother didn't like to cook, and she often just forgot about meals entirely.

Her parents squeezed past her to sit at the table, and her father fingered the newest painting on the walls. "Nice. I didn't know moose like to go sledding."

"Neither did he," Meg said with a smile. She poured some drinking water into a pot on the burner and used a lighter to get it going since the flint had long since worn out. She pulled two mugs from the drying rack and rummaged through a cabinet to find some green tea for her parents. All the boxes in the cabinet were still jumbled, but if they noticed, they didn't say.

"It looks like your mother and I will be going to Burma in a month."

"It's going to be so exciting! They are building an orphanage there. So many orphans, thousands of them, from the flooding and the warfare. It's just awful."

Meg adjusted the flame on the burner and swallowed down the worry that always came along with her parents' plans. "Are you going alone?"

"No, we'll be part of a team. We're going to spend the next month doing a tour of churches in South Dakota, raising funds and getting ready."

Her mother laughed. "Just when we thought we'd gotten every vaccine we could get, it turns out we have to get boosters."

"Where will you be staying?"

Her mother shrugged, a peaceful smile on her face. "It always works out. Something always works out."

"Where is Mark? What will he be doing before the dorms open up?"

"He's been staying with some friends in Cody. Nice folks. He set up the computer for a camp there, and when he's done he's planning to stay with Jacob and Catherine."

Meg nodded without comment. A decade younger than her, her little brother would be going to college a year early. It made sense. In many ways he was already raising himself. She worried about him, and these last few days without Internet access had been the longest she'd gone without sending him an e-mail or text in years. "I was really hoping he'd be here."

"He might still come," her father said. "He's just very busy. You know how he is. In fact, he's a lot like you. I wish you two could take a little more time to relax."

Meg didn't want to have this discussion again. She wished things were different for Mark, that he wasn't on the run from home to home, living mostly with his face in the computer and always speaking in terms of video game metaphors. She wished his parents spent a little more time with him than they did saving the world. Meg closed her eyes. Of course homeless orphans in Burma would need her parents more than a seventeen-year-old almost-man. Anyone could see that. But where was the line? Every parent in the extended Parks family drew it differently. Her parents didn't draw much of a line at all.

For no particular reason other than a sudden desire to throw a wrench in the works, Meg faced her parents and said, "I published a children's book."

"Oh, really?" her father said.

"Honey, I'm so happy for you! Can I see it?"

"I sold my last copy. I'm supposed to have more waiting for me when I get home."

"That's great, sweetheart," her father said. "You'll have to send one to us when we get a post office box in Billings. We'll be sure to let you know what it is when we get settled."

And that was that. She poured the hot water and some honey in her father's mug and hot water and milk in her mother's, and they went on to talk about the project they would be working on and how they planned to get clothing for the kids past a million impenetrable barriers. Meg tried to listen. Her heart hurt for the kids, children with no mom or dad and very little medical care. Although she tried not to, she was thinking, why did I wait to tell them about the book?

Because they don't really care. It sounded petulant, but in a way it was true. They were happy for her, they wanted her to be happy, and she knew they loved her very much. But her parents carried so much in their hearts that she always shared time there with other things. And when those other things were starving, dying, and persecuted . . . well. Publishing a book meant nothing compared to helping orphans, and she knew it. But the child inside of her wanted something else. Fanfare. Tears. Hugs. Something.

And if she'd gotten it, she would have been embarrassed, and she would have felt guilty.

"Margaret, is your little book a Christian book?"

Meg bit her lip. It was to her, but not the way that her mother would want it to be. "No."

"Oh." Her mother took a sip of tea. "This is wonderful, Margaret. Thank you for making this for us."

Her mother's hair was so gray, and she seemed too young for it. She remembered seeing her mother each fall of her life and feeling shocked at the change in her. It felt as if her mother died a little each summer while she was away, and it had frightened her. It still did. She wanted to ask her mom and dad about retirement, health insurance, having a little apartment of their own where they could retire when they weren't strong enough to travel the world any more.

"God supplies our needs, Margaret," her mother said. "I see that worried look on your face. It's not your job to worry about us, honey. We step out in faith, and He does the rest."

"I know. But you can't keep this up forever."

"And when it's time to stop, we will stop, and He'll find a place for us," her father smiled.

"Margaret, you know I don't like to tell tales," her mother said, and it was true. "I just wanted you to know that I heard Leah had mixed feelings about her maid of honor coming back. Catherine said last night that you did a great job of smoothing things over. I just wanted to tell you that I'm very sorry that you won't get to be the maid of honor today."

"I'm okay, mom. This way I just get to enjoy the company and have a nice time."

"Well, we are going to head up. We have the big tub in the back of the truck."

"The big tub?"

"Oh, you didn't know? Joshua promised Leah a bubble bath." Her mother laughed. "He's very excited about heating up the water for her like in the olden days."

"And," her father added with a wink, "we also have three of Catherine's biggest pots and two extra propane tanks, and I've heard he's got a fancy new oven or grill or something. So it's not quite like in the olden days."

"No, thank goodness," Meg said. "But it's still sweet. I did wonder how she was going to get all dolled up for today. She said she was going to stay up here all weekend. She was determined."

Her parents stood up to go, so she backed out of the way. "We're going back down to town for a while after we deliver the tub and pots," her mother said. "Do you need anything, honey?" When Meg shook her head, she added, "Well, we'll see you then. And maybe you can tell us a little more about your book." She got hugs from both of her parents, and they left.

Meg crawled back onto her bed to get a glimpse of

them leaving. She had wondered about them saying they were driving a truck, and as they backed down the road she recognized it. It was Uncle Jacob's truck they were driving. She wondered what that meant about their old Subaru. Maybe it had finally given up the ghost.

She collapsed onto the bed. Although they didn't ask outright for funding for their mission work, the request was always there. They would ask that she pass on information about their work to her friends. If they met her for coffee Meg always paid the bill. And while they had homes when she was young—one after another—it seemed that they had trouble staying put for even a couple months at a time. Mark wasn't bothered; he seemed to always have a friend's house to go to. Why should it bother her so much?

She buried her face in her pillow and moaned. She hated worrying about her own finances and not knowing if sooner or later she would be paying for her parents as well. There was a lot more to worry about, too. What if they were seriously injured in Burma? What if they were captured and someone had to go to Washington and plead for the government to rescue them? Or what if Mark got in trouble? Her parents seemed to think he was an adult, but he wasn't. He had spending money from his computer work now, and time on his hands. What if he got into drugs?

And what about her? There were only so many jobs for muralists, especially one who specialized in cute and funny. She was saving her income from the book, but that was less than what she needed to fix the Jeep and the bent axle on the trailer. Which was now probably cracked. Meg packed a pillow over her head.

There was another firm knock on the door. Meg was sure it was her parents stopping by again on the way down. She pulled the pillow off her head, tossed off the blanket, and opened the door. "Is everything all right?"

"Well, no, not really," Brie said. She was standing on Meg's doormat in her very stylish leather coat and her hair pulled into the perfect updo, where just the right amount of hair went rogue and broke free, framing her face. Pretty blue eyes. And the movie-star smile.

Behind her was Gage, carrying a piece of leather luggage that clearly didn't belong to him. He glanced at Meg once and looked back down. He looked guilty, Meg realized. Guilty as a puppy dog with a chewed-up shoe in its mouth.

Meg backed up. "Come on in, Brie," she said. "It's still cold out there." Brie came in and looked around nervously, as if there was no safe place to stand or sit. Behind her Gage pushed the luggage onto the floor and then motioned down the road. "I have the Monster running." Then he ran like a scared rabbit.

"I'm so sorry we woke you." Brie was examining the walls and trying to look like she wasn't. "My goodness, the people who had this trailer before you must have loved Mooses." Then she turned around. Without her blanket around her, Meg was standing in all her flannel pajama glory. Fluorescent orange flannel with a pattern of moose drinking coffee and reading papers. Brie gave her a sheepish version of her big smile, eyebrows raised. "And you do too, I see! Very cute. Where did you get those?"

"I don't remember," Meg lied. She really couldn't imagine that Brie was going to run out to find the same set of pajamas. Besides, the pant legs would be too short on Brie, she was sure of that. Meg thought about how she must look, and what her hair must look like, and really wanted to have some time alone to feel bad about it. But she politely said, "So what's wrong? Is it something I can help with?"

"Well, someone just came up with this big metal tub . . . like some sort of livestock water tank, I think, and Leah's all excited because she's going to use it as a bubble bath. Right in the middle of the bedroom, no less, because there is no bathroom. But you probably already knew that, that's why you must be here in this thing."

"It is more convenient." That poor little outhouse up by the cabin was probably getting a workout this weekend.

"So Leah thinks it's going to take forever for the guys to get the water hot. And then they have to drain it out the window with some sort of tube, use that crazy pump to get more, and then heat water for a bath for me. It will take forever, and all the water is coming right out of the ground. So Gage told me you had a shower . . ."

"He did?" Meg wondered how that topic came up and exactly what he had said. Did he tell Brie that she was barely covered by a towel when he figured that out?

"Yes, he did, and I know it's a strange thing to ask, but I just can't stand the thought of . . . um . . . is this city water in your camper?"

Meg was a little taken aback. The woman couldn't possibly think she was hooked up to plumbing here. "I filled up the tank at a water provider in town."

"Oh good! I was wondering if I could use your shower. I could go down to Joshua's parents' place, but it's a good two-hour drive there and back and Leah doesn't want to go. I just don't think I should miss any more time here. So if I could take a quick shower here, I could get it over with and spend my time getting ready with her, instead."

Meg's shoulders slumped. It was a perfectly reasonable request. "Of course you can. It's a little tricky, though, so I hope you can take a very quick shower. You only get about three gallons before the water turns cold." And then it would take another hour to heat back up, and she wasn't sure how many more showers and flushes she could get out of her limited supply.

"Three gallons should do it." Brie smiled, and Meg wondered if she had any idea about what she was saying. There was another knock on the door, and Meg opened it to find Gage with a big, fluffy, green towel in his arms again. Meg couldn't help but smile.

"I already have one, remember?"

Gage gaped like a fish breathing air, and from behind her she heard Brie say, "Oh, thanks, Gage! I almost forgot. Thank goodness you remembered."

This towel wasn't for her. Meg clenched her teeth against the feeling of embarrassment. Of course he hadn't brought her anything, he was too busy bringing things to Brie. Gage pointed down the road and vanished again, and she gratefully closed the camper door.

Brie started to unpack the large leather case, which seemed to be full of nothing but toiletries. One of the first things she pulled out was a large hair dryer. "Would you believe they don't have any power up there? Thank goodness you have this thing."

Meg finished attaching the hose and strung it out the window. "I have a twelve-volt station. It's basically a car battery with different plug-ins on it, but it won't last for long if you use something like that hair dryer." She reached under the table and lifted up the power station. The car battery inside made it very heavy, so she set it on the cushion instead of her table. "You can use mine."

Brie looked shocked. "I have two curling irons and a hair straightener, too. It never even crossed my mind. Now what am I going to do? And I wasn't going to do anything until I had my dress on, because I'll mess up my hair."

Meg looked lovingly at her power station. "You can take it with you after you shower," she said. It was like giving up a friend.

"Oh, thank you!"

Brie had bath slippers and a robe in her bag, and while Meg went out to hook up the shower head to the hose, Brie changed. She heard the motor of the Monster and even smelled the exhaust, but it looked like Gage had driven it down the old logging road, away from her camper. Well, that was polite. Maybe he wouldn't walk in on Brie and then get mad at her.

Brie came out, the big green towel in her hand. She stepped gingerly on the dirt in her fluffy slippers, and when she peered around the corner of the camper she smiled, but her face was full of worry. "This is it?"

"I'll head back inside now and turn it on. Remember, you don't have much time. If you have to shave or anything like that, use this lever to turn off the water. It won't really turn it all the way off, but it will at least slow down the flow and save your hot water." And save some water for me, Meg thought.

Once inside, she turned the faucet to the perfect place. "It's hardly coming out," Brie called through the open window. "Is something wrong?"

The little DC pump was working its heart out. "No, that's all the water pressure there is."

"Okay, thanks!" Brie called bravely.

Meg sat down on her bed again and listened to the pump run. After a very long time she heard the water slow down. She shook her head. So much for saving water. She waited. "Oh, brrr," Brie said softly from time to time. Then the water started up again.

Meg put her hands over her eyes.

"Oh!" Brie exclaimed. "Oh! Meg, can you turn up the hot water a little?"

Meg adjusted it all the way to hot. "That's it, Brie, I'm sorry."

"Thank you . . . oh! Oh my . . ."

The cold water certainly sped things up for the maid of honor. When Brie finally asked for the water to be turned off, she said it through chattering teeth. "Come inside," Meg said, and she turned up the heat a little. Brie opened the door. Beneath the enormous green towel on her head, she looked pale and frozen. "Here, stand in front of the heater for a minute."

Brie did as she was told, and in a little while she started breathing normally again. Then she gave Meg a pleading look. "Is there somewhere I could change?"

Why hadn't Meg changed into real clothes while Brie was showering? Meg smiled and tried to slip past Brie in the narrow hallway, managing to accidentally knock her towel-first into the bathroom door. "Oh, I'm sorry. Here, I'll go outside, Brie. I have to go . . . um . . . check something anyway." She grabbed her blanket, shoved her sock-covered feet into the flip-flops by the door, and left her camper.

It was warming up outside, and the birds were singing, but it was still plenty cold out. She had said she would check something, so she tried to find something to check. She looked back at the camper. No, all the curtains were open, so wandering around the camper would be creepy. She headed for the Jeep. And once she cleared the Jeep, she couldn't help but notice the

Monster down the track, smoking. It looked as if Gage was in the driver's seat, waiting, and as soon as he saw her he started backing up. "She's not ready yet," Meg called from her position next to her Jeep. He didn't hear her, so she reluctantly came around the side of the old Hummer and said loudly, "She's not ready yet."

He nodded. Then he turned the ignition off. She thought it was extremely polite of him, since the Monster only started when it felt like it.

"Sorry," he said. "When I saw you, I thought . . . I mean, you're still . . ."

Still in orange flannel pajamas and a blue blanket, of course. "Brie's changing clothes right now. She's going to finish getting ready up at the cabin."

"I'm sorry about all this," he said. "Things are pretty crazy right now. Maybe after the wedding I can . . ."

Head home to Texas, Meg thought. At the same time, Brie fit her towel-wrapped head through the door of the camper and called, "Gage, honey, could you please help me with all this heavy stuff?"

Gage opened the door and Meg got out of his way. He went into Meg's camper and came out with the power station and a suitcase, and Brie came out with her towel still on. "Thank you so much," she said to Meg, touching her arm as she spoke. "You've saved the day."

Meg watched as Gage loaded everything onto the Monster. Just before he set the power station in place he turned to her with a questioning look. "You sure?" he said.

She nodded. "She needs it for her hair."

Gage looked like he was going to say something else. "Is it ever going to warm up today?" Brie said, and he took the hint and got in the Hummer instead. Meg gave a halfhearted wave and headed back to the camper.

Behind her she heard Gage cranking the ignition and the Monster's refusal to cooperate. She waited by the door. And waited. The ignition sounded a lower tone now. The battery must be drawing down, she thought. From a whine to a growl, the Monster sounded slower and slower until she couldn't ignore it anymore.

Meg had jumper cables. For that matter, Joshua probably had them too. She turned around and walked back to the Hummer. Just at that moment Brie turned to see Meg. She probably sensed the impending doom, too.

On the last, low growl of the ignition, it caught.

Meg was standing in exactly the wrong place as a black belch of exhaust smoke blew out all over her. Brie put her hand on Gage's shoulder and called out something over the furious sound of the engine, perhaps even saying that Meg had been sprayed by the four-wheeled skunk. But Gage hadn't seen it. He was celebrating the fact that he'd started the Hummer. He kicked it in gear and headed down the old logging road. Meg coughed. She hung her blanket over the Jeep to air it out and headed back into the camper.

As soon as she was inside she took the coffee percolator off her little drying rack and poured water into it from her water bottle. The routine was so familiar that her hand went to look for the clear plastic insert that fit in the top before her mind knew it had. Her hand didn't find it, though. It was not on the drying rack.

There was no perking coffee without the little window it perked into. Everything would just pour all over her range top without it. She looked on the counter, which was only about a foot long, then the table, then the floor. She searched again and again. It was a tiny camper; where could it have gone? She searched the bed, the steps and ground outside the camper, the bathroom, her bed. And did it all again, over and over. It was beyond frustrating, and although she wasn't prone to them, she had some nasty words ready to go at a moment's notice.

She searched the medicine cabinet for no good reason, and when she closed it again she saw her reflection for the first time that day. She had washed her face last night, but she hadn't gotten all the mascara off and she looked like a raccoon. Her hair was utterly flat, it had a rat-sized rat in the back, and she had a feather stuck in the front. It probably came from the down throw on her bed, but that didn't make it any less weird looking. And although she could only see the top of her pajama top, it was abundantly clear that it had been buttoned up wrong. She looked down. Sure enough, the hems at the bottom of the shirt were shifted one button off.

Meg took one step to get out of the bathroom, one look at the coffee-less percolator, and decided to go back to bed.

The problem with being facedown in her pillow was that her mind was free to calculate how much water she had left. It wasn't much. She had lived out of the camper so often, over several years, and she knew its limitations better than her own. There certainly wasn't enough for a shower today and Monday morning, when she was supposed to go to her next job location. Something would have to go.

Well, at least she wouldn't be wearing a green dress that was too tight and too long for her. It was a blessing that she didn't have to wear the matching shoes. And now she probably didn't have to wear heels at all.

She propped herself up on her elbows. It would be pointless, dressing up now. She could wear her best backup: nice shoes, dark jeans, and a stylish top. She'd wear her hair back in a ponytail. She wasn't in the wedding party, and there was no one to dress up for now.

She thought about the moment the exhaust fumes had come out of the Monster, the moment Brie put her hand on Gage's shoulder. He had not seemed surprised. It seemed to her like a very natural gesture for both of them. The same was true when Brie asked for help with her bags and he willingly and quickly came over, as if it were his job every day.

Then there was the "Gage, honey." It certainly seemed that those two knew each other very well. They were used to saying sweet words and touching. Meg went facedown in the pillow again. Why did it bother her so much?

Why should the fact that he wouldn't push his nosy, cupboard upsetting, axel breaking, oversized self into the rest of her day bother her?

She loved how it felt racing through the water with him, and she wanted to know how he got to be so fast. She loved how he danced, how he never seemed to worry about looking foolish. And he was so, so good looking. By itself that was a silly reason to think about a guy, but something about the way God had configured his face, especially his grin, just made her guts twist inside of her.

He made her head ache, her skin flush, and her blood pressure go up. "He's kind of like a virus," she mumbled into the pillow.

Joshua chose him as his best man. What did that mean? It meant that he was either a very good guy or he was one of Joshua's rescue cases. It could mean anything. But he could quote her book by heart! And his unbelievable honey-brown eyes lit up when he talked about his nephew. There was something about a man who didn't just love his nephew but actually seemed to enjoy his company. He wasn't too cool for kids. He wasn't too cool for contra dancing, getting dunked, or being someone's valet. And for a girl who had never once in her life been the cool kid, that meant something.

Did she make up the way he looked at her, or did he just look that way at every girl? Or at every maid of honor? No. He had singled Meg out, but there was something more between him and Brie, and from the moment she had showed up, Meg had become just another wedding guest to him. Was Brie his girlfriend? If so, why hadn't they arranged flights from Austin together? It didn't matter. Anyone who was attracted to a woman like Brie couldn't find much about a girl like Meg to keep his attention.

And what was worse was that she was a "good girl." The longer she went without casual dating, the less she found she wanted it. She didn't really get the whole dating thing at all. It was confusing, time-consuming, and expensive. From what she heard, from a man's point of view that made her frustrating, demanding, and unrealistic.

Meg was gazing down the barrel of her thirties with no home, no kids, no prospects, and she expected the right man to materialize out of thin air. Where? In her camper? Someone like Gage didn't fit there, anyway.

Meg's heart stopped for just a moment.

There wasn't any place in her life for a man, unless he was an unmitigated slacker. He would have to follow her around from job to job or sit at home in her apartment waiting for her. She didn't have a lawn for a man to mow or a mortgage a man could pay. She paid her own bills, however stingy her life was. She didn't have any kids that needed a dad. She didn't even have a dog for him to walk. And except for weddings, she didn't need a dance partner.

Every single thing in Meg's life was something she could handle just fine alone. And as clearly as she could see her own paintings on the walls, she knew that if she made room for a man, she'd have to live a life that she couldn't handle alone. He'd have friends and family of his own. They'd have neighbors, bosses, and a church family, and she couldn't do as she pleased when she pleased. Just the thought of a mortgage payment made her want to hyperventilate. What if he wanted four dogs?

She wondered if Gage liked dogs. Then she caught herself wondering about Gage and marriage all at the same time and she moaned again, loudly enough that she hoped it would chase the thoughts away. Oh, she wished she had some coffee.

Meg stayed that way for a long time, trying not to think about anything at all, and let the last few thoughts she'd had settle down and stop yelling at her. After her mind quieted down, she finally sat up on her bed and took stock of the situation.

In order of importance, she wanted coffee. There were so many other worries that she could hardly keep them straight—her parents, running out of water, her brother, her next job, that pesky Texan and the lovely maid of honor, and more. But as she tried to sort it all out, she knew that more than anything else, she wanted to have an idea for a second book before she told anyone else about the first.

She did not want to leave anyone, including Gage's nephew, expecting something she couldn't provide.

There was a time when Mouse the Moose stories popped up in her head daily. She would think about difficult things kids dealt with—whether it was something that happened to her or a kid she knew—and just write. Like today. She would imagine Mouse had been invited to a party by the new kid at school, but when the new kid spent the rest of the school day with a different friend, Mouse felt left out and didn't want to go to the party.

Because that's what she wanted, to just stay in her trailer and skip the party. She pulled out her sketch pad and drew Mouse trying to peek around a tree. He leaned so only one eye showed, but of course his antlers stuck out on either side. He was trying to look at his friend playing with someone else. Brie, her name was. She drew a wheel of cheese, giggled, and then erased it because it made her feel vaguely guilty. Long, red hair . . . of course, she's a fox. Because she's a fox. Meg laughed out loud. She's fast and sleek and Mouse would feel like a big doofus next to her.

What did the new kid look like? Well, there was no Montana critter taller and gawkier than a moose, and that species was already taken. But he could swim, too. There were no dolphins in Montana. She could make Gage a northern pike, a big, ugly, hook-nosed fish with sharp teeth. No, that made her feel guilty again. He had amber eyes and he was fast. Maybe he would be a wild mustang. She drew him cavorting in a creek.

He was beautiful. She'd certainly want him as a friend.

She glared at the drawing. Mouse the Montana moose would feel stupid and want to stay home from the wild mustang's party. If it were her child reading this story, if her child had a wounded heart, would she want him to stay home or go to the party? Kids could be mean, whether or not they were trying to. Certainly they were cliquish. She'd want two things: for her child's heart to be safe, and for her child to be brave.

She'd put him in his favorite shirt, let him wear his favorite slippers, cover his face with mommy kisses, and give him a cell phone so he could call her every five minutes. Meg put her head in her hands. No wonder she didn't have any kids. She'd warp them.

Mouse would retreat to his favorite bog. He'd have a moss and cranberry sandwich. The eagle might fly by. That eagle knew a lot, because she had raised twenty-seven chicks. She would tell him that he just might have fun at the wild mustang's party, and he should give it a try. And he should bring something that made him happy, so he would be happy even if everyone else was boring.

Nothing makes a moose happier than moss. So he would dunk his antlers in the water and come up looking slimy and green. Or he would look like a Christmas tree.

That's it! It would be a Christmas party. Mouse would look silly, but he'd pick up cranberries, mistletoe, icicles, and all sorts of other decorations on his way to the party. By the time he arrived he would be the life of the party.

And it would turn out that the fox liked cranberries and the wild mustang liked moss, and Mouse would share his snacks with them. Meg could see it now. There would be things the wild mustang liked to do with the moose, like run fast and jump fences. Maybe the fox and mustang liked their own games together, and the book would make it clear that it's okay to have different friends and share different interests.

Meg frowned. Clearly the book had a life of its own. It didn't have anything to do with her own situation. She had no plans to wear moss to the wedding, it wasn't Christmas, and it was definitely *not* okay if the wild mustang liked to cavort with the fox once in a while.

She looked out the window and felt grumpy about the wedding, and when she looked back at the table she saw it covered with drawings. There was a story here, and images that made her smile. When Monday came, she would have something to tell her publisher. The sense of excitement and relief bubbled up inside of her. It came out first as a prayer of thanks, and then it ended up being a full-on Snoopy from Peanuts happy dance as she sang, "I have a story! I have a story!"

Having that worry lifted from her shoulders was even better than drinking coffee.

She remembered then that she had a couple instant coffee emergency packets in her cupboards. She boiled the water, made a cup, smothered the nasty taste in hazelnut syrup and milk, and enjoyed it. The taste of coffee made her remember her Bible. She plopped it down in the middle of the Mouse drawings and took her time reading. After a little James and a little Proverbs she was feeling imperfect but peaceful. She set down the empty cup and opened the one tall cabinet in her camper. It was ten inches wide and held all long things, including a broom, an extension grabber, a nice skirt, and one dress with the tags still on it. She pulled out the dress and hung it over the door to get a good look.

It didn't look like much on the hanger. It was gray with short, cap sleeves and a subtle silk ruffle along the neckline. But the fabric was gorgeous, rich and soft, and it fit like it was made for her. She couldn't wear hiking boots with it. And she couldn't drive her Jeep up to the crowded meadow in front of Joshua's cabin. She stared at her boots, which were tucked under the edge of her bed. She should wear them with jeans, and a ponytail, something nice and simple.

She thought of Mouse hiding behind the tree. That's just what she would be doing if she wore that.

The alternative was the dress, this same one that called her when she was out shopping for a nice performance fleece jacket, luring her in with its flawless fit, fetching drape, and vintage styling. And heels. Vintage patent leather shoes with an interior made like tennis shoes. What brilliant person thought that up? They were so comfy she had purchased the red ones, the only color in her size. She imagined herself hiking up the steep, rocky road. They would be scratched. She'd probably get sweaty, get bitten by horse flies, and then break an ankle.

Meg needed another cup of coffee. By the end of it she decided that taking a shower didn't necessarily commit her to wearing the dress, it just bought her a little more time to decide. So she took a very quick shower and put on some shorts and a T-shirt.

Now what about her hair? Brie had taken her power station, and now she had a travel hair dryer with a DC plug and nowhere to plug it in . . . except the Jeep.

That was how she came to be sitting in the driver's seat with her Jeep running, stereo on, singing into her knees with her head upside down and out the open door. And when she flipped her hair back and looked up, she saw Gage standing about ten feet away with something large and blue on his shoulder.

He was grinning at her, and just the look of it made her blush from her hair to her toes. She was about to admonish him about something, like sneaking up on her or spying on her, when she realized he was carrying a five-gallon plastic bottle of water. Her jaw dropped. "That's heavy," she stated.

"True," he said, his voice strained. "May I please dump it in your water tank so I don't have to carry it anymore?"

Meg finally jumped into action. She hurried as fast as her flip-flops would go to the inlet, which was right next to the door of the camper. Then she got out of the way. He set the bottle down on the ground and stretched for a second. "It's not bottled water. I just used an empty one and filled it from the well, if that's okay. I figured you might be getting a little low."

"That's perfect," she said. "Did you carry that all the way down from the cabin?"

"Nah," he grinned. "I hitched a ride to the end of the road; someone had to go down to their car in the valley." He picked up the awkward and heavy bottle and poured it into the tank. "It's not much," he said as the last drops went down.

"Five gallons goes a long way for me," she smiled. "Thank you so much." Ah, amber-brown eyes, lashes longer and darker than a boy's ought to be, and hopelessly messed-up dark hair. What a combination. He smiled right back at her for half a second, and then he cleared his throat, stepped back, and shoved his hands in his pockets.

"I'd better go. When are you coming up? There's extras for lunch if you want something."

"No thanks. I was going to stay out of the way a little longer."

He nodded, picked up the bottle, and said, "You're not in the way. For Leah, I mean. Well, you're not in my way either, if you want to be up there. Not that I'm telling you that you have to, of course. But you knew that. Okay, I'm leaving now." He turned and headed briskly back down the logging road.

That was strange. When Meg was done watching him go, she went back to finish her hair. She had the little converter for her phone charger in the Jeep, she realized, and she could plug in the little travel set of hot rollers if she wanted to. That wouldn't be committing to anything. She could still wear curly, tousled hair with jeans.

In the back of her mind she was thinking: He had brought her water. And he had even walked part of the way. When those thoughts threatened to bring on another happy dance, she remembered something: that wild mustang was on his way back up to the fox.

It was getting hot, especially for the mountains. Meg had eaten a small lunch, done her hair and makeup, and tried on the dress. One look in the mirror and she knew she was going to wear it. There were only as many chances in her life to get dressed up as there were friends and family members getting married, and this was the only wedding this summer.

She put on the heels and dropped a jacket into her messenger bag. On her way out the door she remembered the wedding present.

It was heavy with a rustic wood frame, so she slung the bag back over her shoulder, hefted the painting into her arms, and started down the old logging road. She thought about something she had read in Proverbs that morning: "When you walk, your steps will not be hampered; when you run, you will not stumble." However inappropriately, it had made her think about this very road. Of course it was meant to be metaphorical, but here she was, on a real road, carrying a big painting she was beginning to think was a stupid idea for a present anyway.

She hadn't stumbled yet. She made it to the end of the logging road and stood there, staring at the driveway to the cabin, which was much steeper. One of the guests, maybe even a friend, would drive by, or she might have to switch shoes and walk it. As she wondered just how literal "stepping out in faith" had to be, she heard a car engine. It sounded like her Jeep. Her heart raced a little and she looked downhill, where the sound was coming from.

Around a bend came the exact twin of her old Jeep. And at the steering wheel was her brother, Mark.

After she put the wedding gift in the backseat and he gave her a hug, he pinned her with a quizzical look. "Did you know I was coming? Because I didn't even know."

"I installed a tracking system on your Jeep," she joked.

He looked at her like he wouldn't put it past her. For all the years between them, they could still have been twins—same pale hair and pale gray eyes. Of course she didn't have the "cool patch" of facial hair on her lower lip. Looking at him, she thought the distance between them in age seemed to have diminished now that he was older. "Are Mom and Dad here?" he asked.

"Yeah, they dropped by my camper this morning."

"Africa time?"

She laughed at the old joke. They never could be sure when they would get phone calls from their parents because their access to phones was often limited. She and Mark liked to joke that they forgot the world had different time zones. "Portuguese, I think."

He started the drive up to the cabin. He was taking

his time, which didn't seem like him at all. "Is the Jeep okay?"

He laughed at her. "I was trying not to mess up your hair. You look really nice."

She grinned. Compliments from brothers were a rare thing, and they were almost always sincere. "So do you. Have you heard about Burma?"

"Yeah, they told me. They were a little worried about where I'd live in the fall, but I have a dorm room grant for the first semester. But after my first semester I can probably get a dorm monitor job, and that would pay for the stuff I don't want to have to pay for."

He had changed, grown up so much. She thought about how much older her parents, especially her mother, seemed after each of their missions. She never thought about how much more grown up their children must have seemed to them. She didn't want that for her kids, to go away and come home to find them changed. She had a good childhood, and Catherine had filled in so many of the empty spaces in her life. But she still didn't want that childhood for her kids.

She thought about that walk God wanted her to take and remembered that he had a different walk planned for each of his children. She hoped hers involved being there after school, day after day, year after year, until her kids were just plain sick of her. She wondered if God would let her off that easy and not make her do something like a mission to Burma.

"You're worrying again, doof," Mark said.

"I am not."

"Liar."

"Okay, I am, a little. I was thinking about Burma and—"

"Well, cut it out. It's not your job to worry about

them, and besides, it makes them happy."

She stared at him like he had just come from Mars. "They do love it." Somehow she'd forgotten that part. "And it isn't my job, is it?"

"This just occurs to you? Remember the 'each day has trouble enough' line? You're not supposed to take on worry that isn't yours. Have you had a head injury lately?"

"Very funny. And I suppose you're a Bible scholar, now." She expected a snarky comment in return but got nothing. He hadn't changed that much, had he? "I was just teasing, Mark," she said.

He looked at her with one eyebrow raised. "What if I am?"

Meg wanted to know what he meant, but they had cleared the top of the road and driven straight into the heart of the party. Mark used the Jeep's clearance to make his own parking place out of the way, and he got out of the Jeep and picked up her present. "Did you paint something for them?" he asked loudly. She looked around nervously, but no one in the wedding party was around to hear him.

"Yeah, do you think that's dorky?"

He shook his head. "Nah. I kind of wish you'd do another painting for me. Or maybe I could just frame your book."

She froze. "How did you know?"

"Internet search. I was thinking about reserving a domain name for you, but you have a website already. It looks awful; you need me to redo it for you. Monetize it. Add links and partner up."

"How long have you known?"

He shrugged like a big twelve-year-old. "I dunno. When were you gonna tell me?"

"Today."

"Why today?"

"Because I've decided to be brave today. I'm wearing high heels, I curled my hair, and I'm going to the party with moss on my antlers."

Mark sighed dramatically. "And you're supposed to be the grown-up one. Where is this present supposed to go?"

She wasn't sure, but they both thought the cabin was the most likely place, and they headed that way. Sure enough, there was a big table on the deck full of wedding gifts, and a couple chairs to catch the overflow. She was looking for a safe place to set it and not finding one when she heard the door creak open. "Pssst! Meg!"

She turned around to see Leah peeking through a crack in the door. "Come here! Oh, hi, Mark! Go away, you can't see me yet."

Mark chuckled and headed off the deck, hands raised in surrender.

Meg didn't realize she still had the painting in her hands until she tried to go through the door and had to open it wider to fit. Once she was in, she turned to Leah and tears sprang to her eyes. She set the painting down and leaned it against her own leg. "You look so beautiful," she said. "Oh for heaven's sake, I'm crying already. I'm hopeless."

"You'd better stop that, crying is contagious!" Leah gave her a big hug. The painting tipped over and landed on the floor with a thud. Meg jumped, but she didn't hear anything crack or tear. "Oops."

"Is that for me?" Leah said. She sounded genuinely surprised. Meg wondered what she would do when she saw the horde of presents out front.

"You have to share with Joshua. In fact, I'm sorry to

say it might be more of a present for him than you. But that's because it has to do with you."

"I can't wait, Meg. I know what I hope it is, so we'll see. And you look incredible. Did you design that dress?"

Meg had to laugh at that. "If I had, it wouldn't have looked anything like this . . . maybe like a potato sack."

"It looks like you. I'm guessing that you'll be a little more comfortable in this than the green dress."

"I will never say."

From down the hall they heard the sharp snap of high heels on wood and Brie's voice saying, "Are you sure you don't want to try this color?" She came around the corner brandishing lipstick. She stopped when she saw Meg and gave what seemed to be a very stiff smile. "Hi, Meg. Is everything okay?"

Brie was stunning. The green dress wasn't tight on her, it actually moved and draped. It was so much shorter on her that her long legs showed well above the knee. The dyed-to-match shoes didn't look contrived, they looked couture on her. She wore a simple gold necklace with a gold locket on it, a gold bracelet, and—the only other accessory—her long, shining, brilliantly red hair.

Meg went from feeling lovely to dumpy in nothing flat. She pushed the thought aside. That kind of comparison was nothing but coveting, and it was wrong. It made her feel wrong. She pushed back her shoulders and smiled. "Brie, you look stunning. That's a beautiful color on you. Now I can't wait to see Cadence's dress. As a matter of fact, where is she?"

"She's in the back with Catherine," Brie said. "She's trying to get her mom to shorten her hem."

"Not likely," Meg and Leah said at the same time. Meg glanced down the other hall. Where were Joshua and Gage?

When Meg heard the door behind them open, she turned to see a thin woman wearing a red sheath dress and lots of jewelry walk in. Meg thought she looked like a woman with an important and public job, some powerful executive whose age was difficult, or even dangerous, to guess. "I had no idea there would be so many people here!" she said, fanning herself with her hand. "I can't imagine why Joshua hasn't put air conditioning in this place. Or toilets, of course."

"Meg," Leah said, "This is my mother, Brittany. Mom, this is Meg."

Meg reached for her hand, and Brittany's cool fingertips barely brushed her palm. "Pleasure," she said. She looked over Meg's shoulder to see Brie. "Look how sexy! You did such a good job of picking this dress out. You and Leah, I mean. You can wear this dress again, for sure. I know a club in Vegas that's difficult for most girls to get into, but the moment they saw you in this, you'd be at the front of the line."

Meg glanced at Leah and saw a stiff smile painted on her lips. She leaned a little closer. "You know, if he had any idea how to describe it, I bet your wedding dress is exactly the dress Josh would have picked for you."

Leah snickered. "I asked him what he wanted a while back. He thought and thought and finally said that it should probably be white."

"He's a big help, isn't he?" She turned to Leah's mother. "Are you going to stay with Catherine and Jacob, or do you have someplace else to stay?"

Leah's mom shot her daughter a sideways look. "Well, that was an option, but I hate to be a bother. I looked into renting a car and driving into Chico, but it is such a long way to go, back and forth. And then I thought, well, the last person Leah wants hanging around on her wedding night is her mother! And since tonight is the first night in our Santa Fe time-share, it seems a shame to spend it in Montana. So wouldn't you know it, these little airports around here actually have some red-eyes. I'm flying to Salt Lake, catching a flight to Santa Fe, and I should be there no later than if I'd been out dancing all night." She laughed lightly. "It's the best of everything. I get to see my lovely daughter get married, and then when everyone else sneaks off to sleep, I'll be having a nightcap in the clouds."

"Mom, remember, there's a service here in the morning. Josh's Uncle Jeffrey will be presiding. I was really hoping you could stay for that," Leah said.

Brie stepped forward and slipped a slim arm around Leah's waist. "Brittany, we would all love it. If you are worried about the flights, I have a travel agent friend who owes me a favor. She can work wonders, even switching airlines."

"No, no, don't worry yourself, I wouldn't want to be a burden. No, you won't even miss me, will you, Leah? I didn't think so, honey. It's going to be a wonderful day, isn't it?"

Her mother hadn't given her a chance to answer one way or the other. Meg saw Brie's arm squeeze Leah a little closer, and she was glad once more that Brie was here. Leah still needed all the people she could get on her team.

And as Meg stood there in a small, awkward silence, she realized just how much she would rather be abandoned for orphans than for a vacation.

The silence was over in a flash. Cadence came clomping and eye-rolling down the hallway in her own green dress, Catherine came after her, and from down the other hallway she heard Gage calling, "Can we come out now?"

"No," Catherine said firmly. "You'll be free to mingle in a moment, but first we have to round up the bride. Leah? It's about time for your finishing touches."

"What finishing touches?"

"Whatever busywork will keep your nerves steady for the next ten minutes, dear. Brie, you are perfection. Cadence, get over it. Meg, you look like a 1940s movie starlet. Brittany, I have some iced lemonade hidden in the back room, would you like some?"

As the other women started to move into the bedroom, Leah turned back and took both of Meg's hands. She looked pale. "Ten minutes."

"And then you'll be one of us. Muah hahaha."

A change on Leah's face made Meg turn around. Jacob was coming closer, shaking his head. "You look like a million bucks, Miss Leah. My son is a lucky man." Meg stepped to the side as Jacob cleared his throat. Very softly he asked, "No chance your father will come?"

"He doesn't really play a big part in my life, Jacob. But that's okay. God's gonna walk me down the aisle, anyway. He plays a *very* big part in my life."

Jacob was not a big talker. It seemed to Meg as if his pastor brother and Meg's own father had gotten all the talking genes, but their eldest brother had missed out on them entirely. He fidgeted and coughed and seemed like he was gearing up for a long time before he began speaking again. "Leah, I don't know for certain, but it seems to me your Father in heaven would like you to have a real hand to hold when you walk down that aisle. I know I'm not your dad. And I'm certainly not Him. But since you will become my daughter today, I sure would be honored if you'd let me be the person holding your hand."

It was the longest speech she'd ever heard from her uncle. "Thank you," Leah whispered. Meg turned to Leah, who was crying, and after wiping away a tear of her own, she started laughing. "Oh, I am such a crybaby."

Jacob did a quick nod, which was a kind of cowboy bow, and headed back down the hallway again without another word. Meg thought it might be another week before he had something else to say.

"I love you guys," Leah said.

"Stop it. I actually have mascara on," Meg said, trying to sop up the extra tears with her fingertips before they fell. "We love you too. I'm so glad you picked Joshua so I get to have you in my family forever."

From down the hall, a little louder and with a trace of a whine, Gage called, "Can we come out now?"

Meg gave her a quick half hug, trying not to mess anything up, and slipped out the door as Leah went into hiding. Outside, the sun was blinding after being in the cool darkness of the log cabin. Meg spotted her brother talking to one of Joshua's prettier friends. Now was probably not the best time to ask him about that cryptic comment he'd made about being a Bible scholar, but she would have a chance to ask him later.

She walked to the edge of the deck. Her parents were talking Uncle Jeffrey's ears off. Jeffrey was in a suit, a real one, with a tie. He looked very official, and she wasn't used to that. She thought of him as Uncle Jeffrey, not a pastor, and somehow he looked a little less fun to talk to this way. And what had he and Gage been talking about, anyway? She got the impression that Gage was the one who had asked to talk. She wondered if it had anything to do with Brie.

She wandered across the deck, scanning the crowd for familiar faces.

The door opening behind her made her freeze. She hadn't gotten off the deck fast enough. The heavy sound of cowboy boots caught her attention and she turned around. All the lovely dresses and fancy suits couldn't hold a candle to one particular Texan in the right pair of jeans, a crisp white shirt and bolo tie, and a suit jacket with a little western flair. And the hat. What was it about cowboy hats? She clamped her jaw shut, hoping he'd just walk by.

Although he had looked like he was in a hurry, he stopped short when he spotted her. He took two steps toward her and stopped again. "Meg," he said, as if she was the last person he had expected to be at this wedding. "You . . . you look . . ." He pointed at the meadow. "I have to go." Then he turned around and left.

In the rush of emotions and embarrassment she felt next, Meg decided that she really, really needed to stay away from that man.

Caleb came out next, loping off the deck. "Head 'em out!" he yelled. Joshua followed, looking pale. He caught sight of Meg, and she met him halfway for a hug. He hung off her like a wet towel. "I'm gonna pass out."

She pushed him off and took him by the shoulders. "If you do I'll tell Catherine about what you did to her rose bush."

"You wouldn't." She could see the smile playing at the edges of his mouth.

"Oh yes, I will. Cowboy up." She gave him a slow motion punch in the arm.

"If this wedding only took eight seconds, I could do it."

She turned him around and shoved him in the back,

and he headed out, giving her a quick smile over his shoulder.

In the meadow, Gage and Caleb were leading people to their seats, rows of camp chairs, wooden chairs, and deck furniture cobbled together on top of a rented dance floor. Down the center of the aisle was a beautiful white runner, and the final streamers of tulle had been strung from tree to tree exactly where Leah and Meg had decided they should be. It looked better than Meg had imagined. God's creation was the chapel, and the details were straight out of a fairy tale.

Meg walked out to the meadow, hoping to sneak in from the outside, but Caleb spotted her. He offered his arm like a pro and led her around the outside of the chairs to the end of the aisle. Ahead of her she saw Gage helping Sonya's mother into one of the better chairs. Meg wished he had been her usher. "Where do you want to sit, Meg?" Caleb asked.

"Wherever you need me to go."

"Okay, we have one empty seat in this aisle, that would help. Just about everyone else is here with someone." She looked at him sideways. He had no idea that he might have said something that would hurt her feelings. And why should she feel hurt? It was just a fact stated out loud. She'd come to a wedding without a friend or a boyfriend. So had Caleb. He didn't care, why should she?

As she sat down between two chatty groups, she knew the difference. She was older. Most of the young singles here had come alone but moved in packs, and at her age the people she knew just didn't get together that way. They had jobs, homes, and families. A girl's night out for her usually included a baby or two—and had to be smoke free, alcohol free, and/or gluten free.

She remembered that in college dozens of people would just hang out at someone's house talking, drinking coffee, and studying now and then. Truth be told, the thought of doing that now made her feel exhausted. She didn't really miss the pack.

She looked around. Her mom and dad were earnestly chatting up a couple sitting behind them, and they had the attention of most of the people sitting nearby. She scanned some more, and a woman she knew through Joshua waved at her. Her husband, who Meg didn't know, waved too. Scanning a little more, she saw Mark. He frowned at her, then pointed at her and to the empty seat beside him. A brother was better than just about any date anyway, so she got up and moved.

The young woman sitting on Mark's other side gave her a look that was something more than curious. Meg introduced herself as Mark's big sister, and the woman's face instantly changed from tentative to cheerful. Meg tried not to laugh. At least she was considered competition despite her advanced age. Just twenty-seven. "I feel older," she muttered out loud.

Mark elbowed her. "You aren't old. You just live like you are."

She glowered at him. "What? I'm hip. I'm an artist, a free spirit, roaming from town to town."

"First of all, no one says 'hip.' You never take a break, you're always worried, and you haven't had a boyfriend since college."

"Boyfriends are overrated." The young woman next to Mark giggled.

Conscious of being listened to, she stopped talking.

A subtle hush moved through the crowd, and Meg heard music start. She recognized some of the musicians from the contra dance the night before, but now they were arranged as a real quartet. The music conjured up flashes of other weddings in her mind, but none of those settings were as bright and cheerful as this.

Caleb walked down the aisle with his mother first. Catherine was smiling, but there were tears in her eyes already, and they were contagious. Meg blinked her own away. Caleb seated her in the front and gave her a kiss on the cheek.

Gage and Leah's mom were next. Leah's mom smiled at every person she passed and even waved at a few. She looked as if she was in a royal procession, and she seemed very comfortable with that. Gage seated her on the other side, without a kiss, and started back down. He looked over the crowd. He noticed her and looked away quickly.

"Did I do something wrong?" Meg mumbled.

"Shhh," Mark hushed. Her seventeen-year-old little brother was a better wedding guest than she was.

This time Caleb walked up the aisle alone, hands clasped in front of him. It seemed to throw him off balance. Gage was next, deliberately slow and looking a little nervous. His hands were clasped in front, too, and she wondered who had given them that bad advice. When Gage turned and looked down the aisle, his face lit up. Joshua was next in the procession.

Joshua looked like the Cheshire cat. He strolled up the aisle like he was in a hurry. Then he turned around and popped up and down on the balls of his feet. He was so ready. Like a few other people, Meg laughed. But then Joshua looked over toward the cabin, and his face changed. He radiated the happy and awestruck look of a man in love.

The crowd stood as one, and since many of the people were taller than she was, Meg missed seeing the bride come out of the cabin. Then again, she'd had her own private showing earlier. Cadence came down the aisle first. Her dress looked a lot like Brie's, only it had cap sleeves instead of a halter top. She was carrying a small bouquet of wildflowers and pink roses and she looked beautiful. Kelly green seemed to be a color that flattered everyone but Meg.

Brie came next, looking as much like a bride herself as a bridesmaid. She was so lovely that Meg heard the murmurs as people tried to figure out who she was. At last Leah started down the aisle. She was wearing a modest veil, but her smile showed through. And so did the look of pride and concentration on Jacob's face. Jeffrey stepped into view and asked who was presenting the bride.

Jacob coughed, stood straighter, and said, "I do." Leah's mom's smiling face never wavered. Meg wondered if she was relieved that she didn't have to walk her daughter down the aisle, or if she regretted not taking the opportunity. If it was regret, it didn't show. Jacob sat down next to Catherine, and the show was on.

Jeffrey's voice carried over the meadow, and with it came the feelings of love and hope that he had for this couple. When Joshua said his vows, he said them loudly, with a smile. Leah's came more softly, but her eyes never left his, and her smile never faded. Meg watched Gage, but he was facing the other way and she couldn't see his face. He looked as if he was staring right at Brie, and that made her stomach flutter. She focused on the bride, and her happiness.

Meg was dabbing at her eyes with a little less success now, and Mark's friend handed her a tissue. That helped. Why did she cry at weddings? Being happy was part of it, of course, but it was something more. There was a tiny hint of melancholy underneath it all. No great new thing comes without some sacrifice. Josh and Leah's life would never be the same, and they would surely face hardships.

She looked over the crowd for a moment. Whether it was nostalgia for their own weddings or a sense of longing for what Josh and Leah had, there was that faint undercurrent visible on their faces. Meg felt the joy of having Leah in her life, but this was also an exclamation point on the end of her youth. Of course the summers with Josh had ended almost a decade ago, but this made them seem even farther away.

He was a married man now, not just her cousin and playmate. He would have his own family someday, and although she would be involved with them, they would not be her family. She felt like she was losing a brother. She looked over at Mark, and when he saw her face he put his arm around her and gave her a hug.

It was amazing how much a loving touch could make a person feel better.

Still, there was truth to her sadness. She felt as if she was standing still. It was time to point herself in a direction, even if it was one she didn't expect, and get going. *God, please help me recognize the doors you want to open for me. Help me to see the plan you have for my life and to take it. Don't let me pass right by in the busyness of my daily life.*

Meg was lost in thought, wondering what the future held for her as she watched the couple exchange rings and Joshua lifted the veil to kiss his bride. The crowd whooped and cheered. Meg stood with the other guests as the newly married couple walked back down the aisle. For just a moment she saw Brie and Gage walk by. Brie was facing her way, one hand in the crook of Gage's elbow and the other resting on his arm, and she was looking up at him with a radiant smile. Gage was facing away, so Meg could only guess he had the same look on his face.

Her stomach did another flip. It was just a quick glimpse as they walked by, but there was something about it that seemed so wrong. Her brain knew they were probably dating. If he was dating Brie and flirting with Meg, he was a jerk. And she wasn't even sure he'd been flirting with her. From what she knew of him, all of the attention he paid her probably had more to do with him being weird than being attracted to her. And he lived in Texas. How convenient that she kept forgetting that part.

But there it was. A sick small feeling that said *wrong*. This wasn't how it was meant to be. She was supposed to be there with him. She was supposed to be the maid of honor, and he was supposed to be her best man. Meg closed her eyes and took a deep breath, hoping to clear the insanity that was running rampant in her brain. It had been so long she'd forgotten that a crush could tweak every synapse, making you believe only what you want to believe.

She rubbed at her temples with her fingertips. This was stupid! She was nervous and half sick just thinking about the man, and the day before she would have given anything to make him leave her alone. Stupid, stupid. "Stupid."

Mark leaned sideways to give her a quizzical look. "You okay?"

She gave him a bright smile and nodded, hoping he would think it was someone else who had been talking to herself like a crazy person. As people filtered out from the seats, Meg realized she had missed Caleb and

Cadence walking down the aisle. She hoped they had gotten over their irritation at having to walk together, since they each thought their sibling was the least cool person in the world.

Meg thought about the hug Mark had just given her, and she had a funny feeling about him. He was different, her little brother. There had always been something special about him. He had a talent for sensing what was going on with other people and for addressing it with compassion. She gave him an admiring look and found him trying to flirt with the girl next to him as he nervously wrung a piece of paper to death. Well, he was still a guy.

The wedding party walking toward the back of the cabin, where the pictures would be taken. The wildflowers up there were beautiful, and the late afternoon light would be perfect. Everyone in the wedding party looked amazing . . . especially the tall Texan. That same man was offering his arm to the fox in the green dress again.

Meg needed to get busy. She saw Catherine by her Expedition and went over to see if she could help change the event from wedding to reception. But Catherine would have nothing to do with that. "You will not mess up your pretty dress," she informed Meg. Meg peeked a look at the notebook in Catherine's hand and saw a diagram drawn of where each food item was to go.

"I didn't know you used cheat sheets," she teased.

"You just wait until you get as old as me, and you'll need them too. Meg, check the front seat for the lighter, would you please?"

Meg checked and found one between the seat and the center console. She returned it to Catherine, and Catherine immediately passed it off to one of her workers. They all did her bidding cheerfully, probably because they had mooched more than a few delicious meals off her. All of Joshua's friends had.

"Mom," Caleb called, "they need you for the photos because they're going to do the family stuff first. You too, Meg."

Catherine issued her last instructions rapid fire and gave Meg a gentle push toward the cabin.

"Aunt Catherine, Caleb must have been mistaken. I thought the formal photos would only be for the wedding party and the immediate family."

Catherine spun on her heel. "And what does that make you, Meg?"

She knew that look. It meant that she would be much better off if she gave the right answer. "Um, family?"

Catherine scowled, which wasn't the worst she could do, but Meg hated it. "Get moving," Catherine ordered. "Besides, I can tell you've been wanting to sneak up there. You've looked that way at least a dozen times."

"No I haven't!" Meg had to move fast to follow the other woman. As she headed toward the back of the cabin, Caleb and Mark joined them. Leah and her mother were being photographed. The photographer, an older and relentlessly cheerful woman, was forcing them into a real hug. At first Leah's mother was very self-conscious about her dress, the angle of her hips, the set of her chin, but for one moment their eyes met and they both laughed, and the camera spun off a few shots. "Good timing," Meg mumbled.

"I thought so too," a voice behind her said. It sent a chill straight down her spine and a blush to her face.

Meg turned to find that Gage had been standing there, pressed up against the back of the cabin and half hidden by the lilac bush. She scowled at him. Catching herself doing it, she wondered if she looked like Catherine when she did. She fought to make her expression neutral, even casual, as she said, "I didn't see you standing there."

He was standing with his arms crossed, one boot heel back up on the cabin, his hat low over his eyes, and a stalk of grass hanging out of his mouth like a western cliché. Standing that way pulled the cuff of his long, dark jeans up just high enough for her to see that his black boots had red roses on the shafts. He caught her looking. "You want a pair, don't you? Well, you're out of luck. They're custom made."

"You had boots custom made with roses on them."

"They look good, don't they?"

She looked him in his amber eyes. Everything about him looked good, from his broad shoulders to the points on the end of his unexpected boots. "Well, you do line dance," she teased. Then he gave her that grin, the one that was an invitation she wanted to accept, and Meg forgot how to speak.

Mark's hand on her shoulder made her jump. "Aren't you going to introduce me, Margaret?" her little brother asked. His voice sounded deeper than usual. She wasn't used to having a man protect her, not since the days Joshua and Jacob kept potential suitors at bay, and she was surprised to find that she appreciated it more than she had back then.

Gage straightened up, tipped his hat back, and held out his hand. "Mark, right? I'm Gage, Joshua's friend. He has told me so much about you. I'm really interested in this youth counseling website you're proposing."

Mark took his hand and shook it earnestly. "Josh has told me a lot about you, Gage. I'm glad to finally meet you in person. Are you interested, really? Because I'm still trying to find support for it." Her brother slipped right past her, and the two men wandered back over to the cabin together. So much for protection, she thought.

The next hand on her shoulder was Catherine's. "Gage is a good one," she said with an encouraging smile.

"I'm not looking for one, Aunt Catherine."

The older woman raised one eye. "Seems to me you've been looking for him all weekend."

Meg remembered that Catherine had planted the seed in Gage's mind to help her park her camper the night she arrived here. This tricky woman was not to be trusted. "He has a girlfriend."

Catherine tilted her head to the side a little, but very little emotion showed on her face. "Did he tell you that?"

"No. I just thought it was obvious, that's all."

"What's obvious? That you are jealous?"

Gage and Mark were walking toward them, and he was staring right at her. Meg's breath caught. Somehow Gage had heard those words over his conversation with Mark, the noise of the wedding guests below, and the directions the photographer was giving. She was sure of it. She would have to remember that the wild mustang in her story had freakishly good hearing. Catherine turned to Gage and crossed her hands in front of her belly as he walked closer. *She wouldn't.*

"Meg was just telling me that she thought it was obvious that you had a girlfriend. Oh, look, it's time to get my picture taken with the newlyweds. Jacob? I think it's our turn now."

Gage's face had a line drawn down between his brows she had never seen before. He didn't deny it, he didn't ask her anything, he just looked at her and it made her squirm. Desperate for a distraction she turned to Mark. "What is this about a counseling website?"

"It's nothing," her brother said. "I've accepted an offer at Trinity Texas College, and I'm working with the counseling department to set up online counseling. The trick is providing multiple access points with hack-proof security. Since I'll be doing a double major in Bible Studies and technological science, I'm kind of their dream come true. I'm getting free room and board and a tuition waiver."

"Texas what?"

"It's a Christian college near Austin. I saw it when I visited Josh down there. Lots of cute girls with awesome Texas accents. And since I'm probably going to be a pastor like Uncle Jeffrey, it seemed like a good move."

Meg felt like she was watching a movie. She was emotionally involved, but the action that went on around her was far beyond her control. How could it be that the Texan knew more about the life decisions of her little brother than she did? She and her brother wrote just about every day, didn't they? How had she missed something so important?

"I didn't know that," she said.

He shrugged. "It's a pretty recent thing. It's been in the back of my mind for a while, but I just woke up last week and knew that's what I wanted to do, so I drove down there and did a job for them at their mountain campus for a weekend. Summer camp, basically."

"You're basing your whole life on a weekend trip?"

He nodded. "Yeah, kind of. I know what I want, and that's it. I know there'll be bugs to work out, but there always are. I'm ready to commit to a college, and that's the one."

"But there are a lot of colleges, Mark." She wasn't

sure why she was trying to talk him out of it. It sounded like this could be a good college, but becoming a pastor was such a huge decision. Besides, so many things that sound good at first turn out to be horrible mistakes. He needed to think about the future.

"Yeah, there are a lot of good colleges. And this is one of them." He gave her a slow punch to the arm. "And it's mine now."

Catherine called to her and Mark, and they made the trek over to the photographer. Meg kept the rest of her questions to herself for now and put a smile on her face. The photographer had a knack for making people feel comfortable, and in no time they were all laughing and trying several funny poses. She might have a stupid look on her face in those photos, Meg thought, but she knew they would be a lot more interesting than the studio shots she had seen from other people's weddings.

Leah asked for a photo of just the two of them, and Meg was happy to be asked. Then it was time for the real bridesmaids and the bride to be photographed, and Meg watched for a while. Joshua stayed nearby with a smile on his face. He couldn't take his eyes off his new wife. Meg wandered a little farther away. Catherine and Jacob had left, probably to manage the wedding reception buffet. When she realized that Gage was headed her way, she ducked into the outhouse.

"Coward," she whispered to herself. Then she whispered, "Hello, Mouse." The first moose she had ever painted was on the wall of the outhouse. She tried to make it look like a happy moose, sticking his head through a window directly over the seat. Catherine had sent her in there to paint the walls blue and maybe put a flower here or there, but that hadn't happened. One of Joshua's buddies had told her a story about having a moose come right up to him as he was busy relieving himself in the woods, and it inspired her, in a way.

She found out she liked painting a moose, and she put another one in a fake pinup calendar painted on the door. That was for Jacob, who had talked about his own father's racy calendars with a mixture of disapproval and fondness. After finishing the outhouse, she drew more moose for the fun of it, and that was how Mouse the Moose came to be.

Meg carefully opened the door a crack. She couldn't see anyone or hear anything but the distant laughter of the girls. She slipped out, closed the door softly, and started out at a fast pace.

"Hey," Gage said from right behind her. He must have been standing next to the outhouse the whole time.

Startled, she spun on him. "First you sneak up on me in the shower, and now this? You have a problem, you know that?"

Gage pointed at the outhouse, shook his head, stuttered, and his ears turned red. "I'm sorry. I'm not trying to do anything wrong."

Meg took her hands off her hips and crossed her arms over her chest. "What did you want?" she said more softly.

"I wanted to talk to you about something. About what Catherine said. I just wanted you to know that I'm not dating anyone."

Meg tried to look as if that couldn't matter less to her. "You're not dating Brie?"

There, a flicker in his gaze. "No." She waited, knowing that wasn't the whole truth. "I used to go out with her. And she got the idea that I wanted to go out with her again, but I didn't."

"And how did she get that idea?"

"From me," he said. He stepped back to look around the outhouse, evidently to make sure that Brie couldn't hear him, and then came back to Meg. "Listen. I don't want to say very much, because it's really between me and her. But I think you've probably already heard that I was a jerk to Brie in many ways. In just about every way a guy can be a jerk, as a matter of fact."

"Did you hurt her?"

"No. Well, yes. I didn't physically hurt her, I'd never do anything like that. But I hurt her heart."

You've probably already heard. No, Leah had not told her anything specific, but Gage seemed to think she had. And Brie hadn't said a single word, not that she had any reason to. Meg wondered if she'd ever heard the words "I hurt her heart" spoken out loud before. He said it as if it mattered to him, as if he regretted it.

At the same time, Meg felt as if she was at the tip of some kind of iceberg. Why say anything to her? Come tomorrow he would be gone, and so would Brie, and they could work out their maybe-get-back-togetherness in Texas. Gage wasn't done talking, though. He took a step closer to her. "I just want you to know that I've done some pretty awful things. I have a past that's, well . . ."

"Checkered," she supplied, using Leah's word.

He nodded.

"Why are you telling me?"

That seemed to take him off guard. "I thought it might matter to you." His amber eyes searched her face, and his shoulders slumped. He seemed to be looking for the right words. "I have a bad reputation and I did a lot to deserve it. I've worked really hard this last year, and although that may not seem like a lot of time to you, I've learned a lot. And I guess I was hoping that you and I could be friends. Because I really like you."

"You don't know me," Meg stated. She ignored the little rush that came with his last words; that was just her silly girl self feeling flattered. "And I'm not sure what to think about you. And since you live in Texas—"

"Oh, Gage's charm extends far beyond Texas." Meg hadn't even realized Brie was there until she stepped around the outhouse, a stiff smile on her face. "It's nice that he likes you, but I wouldn't put too much stock in it. Gage likes all the girls. Don't you, honey?"

Gage looked at her with an expression that Meg could not read at all, and he said nothing.

Brie came a little closer to Meg, and she could see that Brie's neck was flushed red, despite her cool tone of voice. One hand held her bouquet tight at her side, and the other was crossed over her middle. Her French manicured nails dug into her own arm. With a nod of her head she tossed her red hair over her shoulder. "Meg, I see you've gotten to know Gage better than I thought. I guess when I wasn't here he expected you to stand in for me in more ways than one. Maybe stand is the wrong word, though."

Meg felt embarrassed and guilty, although she was sure she hadn't done anything to feel guilty about. With a sinking feeling, she admitted that though she hadn't done anything wrong, Gage had been haunting her every thought. If he was committed . . . What was that about her thinking they were getting back together? She tried to talk and her voice came out sounding squeaky before she got it under control. "I didn't realize you and Gage were dating," she said, hoping to get the truth out on the table.

"Well, we haven't dated for some time, but my phone has been ringing off the hook for the last month.

'We need to get together, Brie. I need to see you right away, Brie. We've been through so much together, Brie, please give me a chance.'"

Meg looked over to Gage. He was looking at Brie with that same unreadable look. It was gentle, even compassionate. Meg felt a little sick.

Brie was looking at Gage, too, but her look was icy. "You thought it was an easy make, me at a wedding, didn't you? But when I got sick you found a backup. Funny, you dropped her pretty quickly when you saw me. Now that you've figured out that I'm not going to be eating out of your hand anymore, you're back to flirting with the backup girl. You are so very predictable."

Meg felt mortified. No one spoke for a while, since those ugly words were more than enough. *This isn't about me*, she thought. "I hope you two can work this out," she said. "For Leah's sake." Then she turned and went back to the meadow as fast as she could in patent leather pumps.

When she was rounding the front of the deck, she heard Catherine call her name. "Are they still taking photos?" she asked.

Meg stared at her dumbly. She had no idea, she'd been too involved in that awful conversation. "I think so," she finally said. Catherine glared at her, her brown eyes endless, and then she crooked one finger at Meg. Like a disobedient child Meg walked slowly around to the steps and onto the deck. By that time Catherine was standing at the door and Meg got another crooked finger. She followed her into the cabin.

"Are you okay?" Catherine asked.

Meg nodded. Catherine was not buying it. "I just had a very weird conversation with Gage and Brie and I don't know what to think, which is stupid, because it's not any of my business."

Catherine nodded slowly as if this made perfect sense. She touched two fingers to her lips. "I see. Well, it's pretty clear what you should do."

"What's that?"

"Give him a chance to explain. Sometimes people have a hard time telling you things, for reasons you might not be able to understand." Catherine gave Meg an even, unflinching look. "Even though it can make you feel like you're not important in their life when someone doesn't tell you things. But you have to give them time, sometimes a lot of time, before you judge them."

Meg felt lower than dirt. "You know about my book."

Catherine nodded.

"I'm so sorry."

"You may not think you're family, Margaret Parks, but I do." Catherine's eyes teared up, and Meg's heart broke. She had never wanted to disrespect everything Catherine had done for her. "I spent at least three months a year with you your whole childhood. I wish it had been more, but the decision was not mine to make. I consider it a technicality that you didn't come from my womb."

Meg was speechless. She realized for the very first time that she had always assumed she was an imposition on Catherine's family, that Catherine's generosity was at the heart of her kindness, not love. At least not that much love.

"I know you have a mother, and she loves you with all of her heart too, but that doesn't change how I feel about you, Meg. So whether it's being in family pictures or telling me about the important accomplishments of your life, you can do what you want. But don't you forget, I have room in my heart and in my life for every little thing you want to share with me, whether it's about stubborn cowboys or an even more stubborn moose."

Meg felt humbled. "Catherine, you've always been a mom to me. But I know you didn't choose to have me, and so . . ."

Catherine waved away the rest of Meg's words. "When you have your own you'll discover you never choose any of your kids. God picks them for you, and you're blessed to have them. He even put you in a place where you could bless two families, and yet sometimes you act like you haven't got even one."

"I'm so sorry. I never wanted you to think I didn't love you, or to be disrespectful." She tried a smile through her misty eyes. "You taught me better than that."

"Yes I did." Catherine smiled. The older woman put her arms around her, and Meg melted in the warmth of that hug. It was just exactly what she needed. First her brother, now Catherine. She would have to do more hugging; it was good for her.

"I told Mom and Dad about Mouse this morning," she said.

"And?"

"They were happy for me." Catherine recognized what Meg didn't say, but she wasn't the type to comment on it. Catherine only sighed. Meg said, "I would like to show it to you, but I sold my last copy."

"I have three here at the cabin and three more in my car," Catherine said. "I'm not going to tell you how many I have at home."

Meg laughed, but the tears finally spilled over. "I'm ruining my makeup."

Catherine fetched a tissue and expertly dabbed her

tears for her. "You look good as new."

"Aunt Catherine, please tell me you aren't the only reason my book is selling well."

She laughed. "No, my dear. And it is selling well, isn't it? Evelyn down at the bookstore looked it up for me, and she told me how to find out its sales rank at Amazon, and so I've been tracking you."

"How did you find out?"

"Your appearance at Crawford Elementary. The librarian is my hairdresser's daughter. But that's another story and has to do with another wedding, and we're here at Joshua's and Leah's wedding. So we have a few things to deal with. I need you to start pouring champagne and sparkling cider. Andrew is going to pop the corks for you. It needs to be you pouring because you remember the approximate age of all our guests. Don't be afraid to card them. Don't you smirk, miss Meg, I'm serious."

Most of the guests had gotten their food and settled down to eat by the time Joshua, Leah, Gage, Brie, and the photographer came around to the front of the meadow once more. Their entrance earned hoots, cheers, and applause. Meg set out the real crystal glasses at their table.

She tried not to look, but she stole one glance. Joshua and Leah were talking about something, and it seemed like Gage and Brie were leaning forward, deep in a private conversation. Meg didn't want to know what they were talking about, and she didn't want to care. *It'll all work out the way it's supposed to.*

With a start she realized Andrew was standing right in front of her, his arm outstretched, a glass of champagne in his hand. "Thanks," she said. "I forgot to get one."

With their job completed she went looking for Catherine. Her aunt was finally sitting down, and there was an empty chair near her. Meg got herself a plate and headed out across the meadow toward that safe place. Catherine looked at her, raised her eyebrows, and said, "You need to eat."

Meg tried a little of everything. It was good, but she wasn't very hungry. She heard the clink of silverware banging against glass. "Excuse me," Gage said. "I would like to say a few words about my friend Joshua."

She glanced over her shoulder. Gage was standing next to Joshua, and although his voice was upbeat he looked uncomfortable. "I was Joshua's roommate when he first met Leah. I remember it very clearly, because I came home to find him pacing like a madman in our living room. I took a seat on the couch and watched him pace for about fifteen minutes. He told me he had met The One. Of course I didn't believe him then. Well, that was a long time ago. A lot has changed for me, and some of that change I owe to Joshua."

Gage stopped there, and for a second Meg wondered if he was actually choked up. But he started again, as upbeat as before. "He and I have been through some hurricanes since that day, but the way he feels about Leah has been rock solid. He's a good man, and he picked an extraordinary girl.

"Joshua and Leah, I know your future holds a whole lifetime of blessings, but I want you to know that you've already been a blessing to your friends. It's been great getting to know each of you, but getting to watch your love grow is even better. May God bless you, and from all of us, thank you."

The cheers rose up, and Meg fished around in the grass to grab her champagne glass and raise it to join in the toast. Gage sat down and Joshua gave him a loud slap on the back. When the noise started to die down, Brie stood up.

If she was nervous she hid it well. She looked poised, with perfect posture. She lifted her glass just a little. "For those of you who don't know me, my name is Brie. I have had the honor of being Leah's friend for more than twelve years. So I thought it only fair that I give Joshua a better idea of what he's in for. First of all, if you want to play cribbage with Leah, you'd better get used to losing. You will never get her to watch the first half of the movie *Bambi,* and she doesn't even want to know what *Old Yeller* is about."

Gage was looking right at Meg. She looked back at Brie as if she hadn't seen him. She wondered what he was thinking behind those amber eyes. She wondered what hurricanes he had been in the last few years. If he'd been in a hurricane, she'd been lost in the doldrums, waiting for a puff of wind to lift her sails.

". . . And so it's fitting that Leah gets her happy ending today, or as I should say, her happy beginning. I love you, Leah."

Another cheer went up, and Meg raised her glass again.

Leah's mother demurred, and Jacob wasn't about to make a toast. That left Catherine or Joshua's little brother and sister, all of whom would have probably dissolved into tears. Luckily for all of the guests, they left it on the good note Brie and Gage had created.

Everyone finished their dinner, and Leah and Joshua cut the cake, gently feeding each other the first piece. That started off another herd, as inexorable as a slow buffalo stampede, that took care of most of the multiple pan cakes. Meg recognized Catherine's signature red velvet cake with cream cheese frosting, and she wasn't about to miss any of that either.

Caleb vaulted over the deck railing and headed across the empty dance floor like a man on a mission. He marched over to the Monster, jangling the keys in the air for effect. He climbed over the door, did whatever magic pedal routine Joshua usually did, and then tried to start the Hummer.

Once didn't do it, and neither did the next four times, although his efforts filled the meadow with black exhaust and the bang of multiple backfires. When the Monster actually started, a cloud of dark smoke rose from its tailpipe. Where was he going? Meg wondered. Rather than heading down the drive, the way the vehicle was pointed, she saw the backup lights come on. Caleb was yelling, "Get out of my way!" and waving his hand.

Chairs parted, and the Monster backed up almost to the dance floor. Then, thankfully, Caleb turned off the engine. With a lot of creaking and coaxing he got both doors open. He held up what looked like a phone and plugged it into the dash. Then, being Caleb, he took a bow and everyone applauded obligingly.

"Ladies and gentlemen, may I introduce Joshua and Leah Parks." He fiddled with something, and the Monster's sound system came roaring to life. After half the people covered their ears he turned it down to a level that was merely loud.

Meg recognized the song in an instant as one of many sappy, tear-jerker Brad Paisley ballads. Josh led Leah out onto the dance floor, gently pulled her into his arms, and danced. They were smiling so hard it was impossible to watch them and not smile as well. As they danced they began to talk and laugh together, and Meg wondered what they were saying. What an adventure they were facing. And although she was happy for them, she felt a little envy creep back into her heart.

Envy was not her favorite feeling. She chased it away by reminding herself she had a good life, an interesting life, friends, and a family who loved her. And she was going to become a multibook author shortly. But whenever she looked at her life, she thought about her future and the uncertainty that came with it. It would be nice to face a future with someone, to talk and laugh in the face of it.

She rolled her eyes. That so wasn't her! She valued her freedom. And she wasn't like her mom and dad, without a single thought about tomorrow, but she didn't want to be the person her brother saw, either. *You aren't old. You just live like you are.* There had to be a happy medium. And whether she found it alone or with someone else, she was going to find it. Just as soon as she knew what it looked like.

When the dance was over, the newlyweds headed her way. Leah found Jacob and took his hand. His face turned a dark red, his expression stern, and he stood up a little taller. For Jacob those were all signs that he was about to complete a task that he considered important. He led his new daughter-in-law onto the dance floor to the strains of an Alan Jackson tune, and he covered every inch of that floor with his impeccable two-step. Good thing Leah knew how to two-step, Meg thought, or Joshua's father would have dragged her around just the same.

When the music changed to some crooner classic Meg knew, it was Catherine and Joshua's turn. In some ways it still shocked her that Joshua was taller than his mother. Now he was a married man, and he was doing a dance step she didn't recognize, but Catherine did. They looked elegant, and when she came off the floor she was glowing with pride in her son.

The next song was an old country classic. Joshua and Leah showed that good two-stepping ran in his family. Caleb and Cadence joined them, doing a swing dance that was good enough to get them the attention they probably hoped they'd get. And then Gage and Brie joined them on the dance floor, making the bridal party complete. Gage pulled the maid of honor into his arms and they danced slowly, swaying from side to side.

Brie's chin was tipped up, although her high heels and her natural height meant Gage was only a little taller than her. She was smiling and talking. Meg looked for something different, some sign of discomfort or awkwardness between the two, but it wasn't there. They almost looked like Josh and Leah in their first dance. For all she knew they were talking about their future, too.

Catherine leaned over. "Margaret Parks. Get that grouchy look off your face or it'll stick that way."

Meg gave Catherine a guilty look. "You weren't supposed to notice that."

"I notice everything, honey. And I suppose you're allowed a little grouchiness, since that lovely young woman is dancing with your man."

"Aunt Catherine! He is not my man."

"Mm hmm."

"You're incorrigible."

"You need to grab this one before he gets away, Margaret." Catherine took a big bite of bread.

"What on earth makes you think he wants to stick around? Or more importantly, why would I want him to? I just met him. He's just a . . ." Meg pictured him standing in her camper. "He's too tall."

Catherine, her surrogate mother, laughed out loud.

"You have a crush on him."

"Oh my goodness. This is not fifth grade." Meg took a swig of water out of her water bottle. She knew Catherine was teasing her, but she was making her feel genuinely irate. She wanted to turn the tables on her. "Just because you think he's cute doesn't mean anyone else does."

Catherine waved her hand in the air. "I already have a cowboy, and one is plenty. I do recommend you get one of your own, Margaret. They can be very . . . handy."

Meg's eyes grew wide. If her aunt meant that as a double entendre, she didn't want to know. She heard Catherine chuckling to herself.

When the next song began, a song with a fun beat that Meg recognized from somewhere, the dance floor was flooded with dancers. This was not a shy crowd by any means.

Catherine took her husband by the hand and dragged him onto the crowded floor, where they did a two-step, of course. Meg laughed as she watched them expertly navigate a younger generation's gyrations. Beyond the dance floor Meg caught a glimpse of Gage and Brie.

He'd leaned his shoulder against the trunk of an old pine, hands shoved into his pockets. Brie was standing with her feet slightly apart, leaning forward just a little, arms illustrating her points with big flourishes. Having heard a little of how sharp her tongue could be, Meg was happy not to be on the receiving end.

When the next song played, Leah gestured to her, and Meg joined a group of women dancing to one of the standard wedding favorites. The heat of the day was lifting, the music was loud and fun, and a long night of celebration was in front of them. Meg danced with the best of them until her high heels demanded a break and her throat, sore from singing along far too loudly, demanded a drink of water.

Meg tried to find her messenger bag, but the chairs were scattered and her bag was nowhere to be seen. She searched for a while and caught sight of Gage and Brie the same place in the darkening forest, still talking.

One of the tables that had held the buffet had been moved around the side of the cabin, and coats and bags were piled all over it. Meg dug until she found her water bottle and then polished off the rest of the water. Having had enough water to quench her thirst, she then poured herself a cup of coffee even though it was late. "Living on the edge," she mumbled. She even added sugar.

"What did you say?"

This time Gage's voice, so close behind her, took her so by surprise that she jumped and spilled coffee over her hand. He took the cup from her and set it in the grass, then he held her hand with one of his and with his other hand pulled a handkerchief out of his pocket and wiped the coffee from her skin.

She stared at the once-white square of fabric. "You have a handkerchief."

"I do."

She looked up into his eyes. The sun was setting and the light was turning orange, and his amber eyes looked like they were made of gold. "I've never known anyone who carried one, except for Jacob," she said. *What a stupid thing to say.*

"And Joshua. He got me in the habit. He said it was the mark of a gentleman." He caught her eye and winked.

"I guess so," she said lamely. She squirmed. She wanted her hand back. His hands were warm and strong and they were making her say stupid things. "Where is Brie?"

Oh, that was subtle. She cringed when she saw him lean back and look at her through narrowed eyes. "Dancing, I think. She and I had a few things to talk about, but you probably guessed that." He folded the handkerchief and put it back in the pocket of his jeans. "I took care of what I needed to do there, and that means I'm free to do what I need to do now."

"And what is that?" she said. She rubbed her now dry hand, wishing the heat, and the tingling that shot up her arm, would vanish.

"I was hoping I could dance with you."

He gave her the grin. The invitation to trouble. Of course a slower song was starting, his timing was perfect. "Um, sure." She turned to head back to the dance floor, but he caught her arm to stop her.

Gage was still grinning. "No, I was thinking we could dance here."

"Here?"

"Well, actually over there, out of the way."

He was gesturing toward a flat, grassy area next to the cabin. No one was there. Her heart pounded uncomfortably against her ribs.

"Is something wrong?" he asked. He was so cool and collected, like lines and clever ideas just flowed off his tongue. She thought about where he had just been, and what Brie had said.

"Do you want to dance here because you're afraid Brie will see us?"

He gave her a long look. He was considering something, and it didn't look good. She wondered if she had been right, and she was hoping she wasn't, although either way she sounded a little like a jealous shrew. Ugh, this man thing was too hard. She almost turned to leave again, but he finally spoke. "I guess I can see why you think that, but you're wrong. Until you get the whole story, you're just going to have to trust me."

Trust him? She didn't even know him.

"I want to dance with you on the dance floor, too, but not to this song. For this song, I want to dance right here, with you." He took her hand again, walked her past the table full of stray belongings, and led her to the shadowed patch of grass.

The air in the mountains shifted in the evening. Gone was the hot, grassy smell. The pinesap and the wildflowers took over, and she could almost smell the cool, watery scent of the creek in the valley below.

Gage took her hand and pulled her close. Her right hand felt small and warm in his hand. Her left hand fluttered awkwardly, first on his shoulder, then his arm, feeling the lean curve of muscle everywhere it landed. Even through the jacket it felt too intimate, and there was no safe place to rest. She let it rest just behind his shoulder and tried to ignore what she was feeling.

With his other hand he pulled her close enough that their clothes brushed together. She looked off to the side, memorizing the leather-trimmed yoke of his jacket and the gabardine. She couldn't look him in the eye.

He swayed gently and stepped slowly, picking the slowest rhythm of the old romantic tune. Was it Sinatra? Was it one of the newer singers? She couldn't place it, but the mood was the same either way. She glanced up at him. His eyes were already on her. In the fading light his tanned face, dark hair, and amber eyes looked almost unreal, like a painting. Only warmer.

Her high heels put her just a little too close to his face, and she looked down. Pressed white shirt collar.

Was that satin under the lapel? His hand felt hot on the small of her back, and the way her dress slid against her skin made her feel like there was nothing between her and his hand.

When she thought things couldn't get any worse, he pressed his cheek against her temple and held her just a little closer.

Meg closed her eyes. He was all around her, gentle and strong, and everything else fell away. She forgot the steps, just felt them leaning together, her bare legs sliding against the denim of his jeans, her head leaning slightly against his, listening to his long and steady breathing. When the song was over they stood still.

Finally Gage leaned back, and she opened her eyes. His face was shadowy, moody. He lifted his hand from her back and with one finger stroked along her jaw line, ending at her ear lobe, light as a feather. She realized he was going to kiss her, and she took a step back and took a gulp of fresh air. What on earth was she doing?

Another song began. Gage's chest lifted with a deep breath, and the grin returned to his face. He gestured toward the dance floor, just out of sight behind her. "Shall we?"

It was another old country classic. She guessed the DJ, who was probably Caleb, was giving the parents a fair shot before the cousins and their friends took over the dance floor again. Her feet were glued to the grass. She stared down at them and saw that in the dark green grass all around her burgundy shoes, tiny white flowers were blooming. It looked like a frosting of snow.

She glanced back up at Gage. "Maybe one more here, first," she said. She couldn't believe she'd said it, but when he grinned at her, she was glad she had. She felt her skin flush from her hair to her toes. He pulled her into his arms again and led her into a slow and close two-step. "I didn't know you could two-step," she said.

"It's required. If you want to be a genuine Texas cowboy, that is." He pulled her a little closer. Their steps got smaller until the dance was little more than a swaying embrace. Meg was lost again, as if all that existed was the feeling of him next to her, the cobalt blue sky above, and the tiny white flowers under their feet.

The song was almost over when Gage froze and she felt his hand tense against her back. She glanced up to see him staring over her shoulder, and she spun around expecting to see Brie. But instead she saw Joshua, arms across his chest, feet planted wide. Meg's heart raced as if she'd just done something very wrong. Had she? She hadn't, had she? Oh good grief, men were so much trouble.

"What have we here?" Joshua said, smiling. Meg figured it was the same look, maybe even the same words, he had used on the friend who was flirting with Cadence earlier.

Gage lifted his hands into the air, surrendering. "Just dancing."

"Did you guys know there's a dance floor back that way?"

Meg glared at Joshua. "Were you on the way to the outhouse, Josh?"

Joshua nodded and started to walk by. "I'll see you back on the dance floor," he said.

Meg watched him go then put her hands on her hips. "It's his wedding. You'd think he'd be too busy to chaperone."

Gage shook his head. "Yeah, but the last thing I want is for Joshua to think I'm doing something inappropriate with you." His hand closed in over her elbow and they started walking toward the other, more crowded dance floor. "He's pretty protective of the women in his life. It's one of his better qualities."

Meg still had the shaky feeling she had done something wrong. There was still a question mark around Brie and Gage, and the fact that he would be leaving for Texas soon. The thought of that chased away any warm, easy feeling she had left over from the dance.

Gage might have sensed her change in mood, because he detoured her toward the cabin. "This way first," he said. He stepped up onto the deck and pulled two chairs over to the railing. Then he jumped the steps down and retrieved two Styrofoam cups of coffee. "They didn't have any honey," he said. "So I put just a little sugar in for you."

He remembered how she liked her coffee. He put the chairs where they had been the night before, before Brie had arrived. She took the cup and sat down. They watched the dancing for a while. Joshua came past, saw them on the deck, then pointed two fingers at his eyes and then at Gage. Gage chuckled.

"Watch it, I think he can take you. He's meaner than he looks."

"Then he hides it well."

Meg looked at Gage, examining his face, the look in his eyes. "You guys are close, huh?"

"When we're not butting heads." He looked back over at Meg. "He's been a big influence in my life."

Meg thought about that for a moment. "He's been in mine, too. How did you meet?"

"We met in school pretty early on, but we were moving in different circles. When we both got accepted to the master's in petroleum engineering program, my advisor said Joshua was looking for a roommate. He was pretty insistent that I call him. I guess he knew I needed to turn things around."

"What do you mean turn things around?"

Gage examined her face as if he hadn't decided she was someone he could talk to. He took a sip of his coffee and made his choice. "I shouldn't have been accepted to the program. My grades were going downhill, my head wasn't in it. I was dating Brie at the time, kind of. But it wasn't just her." He looked back out at the dancers cheering and dancing to a Village People song. "I was on the swim team all four years of college. You wouldn't think that it would mean much to people, it's not like I was a quarterback or something, but for some reason it has its groupies."

"You had groupies," she said. "The rumors I always heard were that swimmers didn't like women very much. And you do have roses on your boots."

He glared at her. "You are just jealous of the boots. You can't have them."

She grinned at first, but her smile vanished as she thought about what he was saying. "I suppose plenty of those groupies were women."

"Yep. Anyone looking for mediocre fame by contact should try swimming." He ran his hand through his hair, harder than she would have expected. It looked to her like he was trying to erase the memory. "You know, all through high school my parents drove me into the city so I could be on a real swim team. Between the training and the extra hour and a half in the car, I was always busy. When college came, and I was on my own. I spent my time wherever I felt like it. Everything was negotiable. Everything and everyone that used to be important to me. I loved school, but I put less and less time into it. By the end of it even swimming didn't really matter to me." He dropped his head, his elbows resting on his knees. "I used to think God was important to me, and my family. I didn't know how right I was."

"Then you met Joshua."

Gage chuckled. "He had house rules. I made fun of him all the time, but in a weird way, a house with a curfew felt more like home to me. Most of all, I got to see that the rules Josh put on himself were a lot more real than the ones he put on me." Gage leaned back and looked up at the sky. Meg followed his gaze and found that the stars were coming out. At the same time, one by one, the solar-powered lights started to come on. They were strung all over the deck, across the dance floor, from tree to tree, and they spiraled down the trunk of the trees that ringed the meadow.

To Caleb's credit, once the Village People finished up, Chris August started playing "Starry Night." It was one of Leah's favorites. Meg took a moment to soak it all in, the scents, the laughter, the "ahs" as if fireworks had gone off. Under the lights, in the middle of the dance floor, Joshua gave Leah a sweet kiss. In the middle of the mountains of Montana—magic.

She looked back over to Gage and found him staring at her, a serious look on his face. "I met Joshua. I was dating Brie, and Joshua met her friend Leah. Joshua knew from the first second that he was going to marry Leah, and he did everything right by her. He used to say it was an investment in his future. It changed things for Brie, too. When she saw how things went for Leah, she began to demand more from me. And I wanted it so much that I tried to go backward, to do everything the way Joshua did it."

Meg's throat felt thick. Her voice sounded hoarse

when she said, "You wanted Brie so much."

Gage looked at her with surprise in his face. "No, Meg. I didn't want Brie, I wanted what Josh had."

Meg thought about that for a moment. She also thought about how mad Brie was. "How long ago did you break up?"

"About a year and a half. But it wasn't a clean break. She thought she loved me, and I wanted to make it up to her, but trying to be her friend just made it worse. I finally quit speaking to her completely." He blew out a long breath. "That was awkward for everyone. Then I heard she didn't want to be maid of honor when she heard I'd be the best man. I've been trying to call her for five months, to get together, to tell her how sorry I am. She didn't want to hear it."

Meg thought about seeing them in the trees, talking for a long time. "Did you tell her?"

"I told her. In the end, she's just going to hear what she wants to hear."

Meg had lots of questions, but not very many of them were something she had a right—or needed—to know. Except one. "Do you think she loved you?"

That brought a long sigh from Gage's lips, and his eyes looked tired and sad. "I've prayed about that a lot. I don't want to think so, because I really messed up. But I can't fix it. So I pray that she finds the right person, so much so that I just don't even matter to her anymore."

Meg doubted that would happen. She'd had crushes that still haunted her from time to time, and she couldn't imagine being so close to someone for so long and then having it end. "I've never broken anyone's heart." She didn't mean to say it out loud.

Gage cocked his head sideways. "Not that you know of. I'd be willing to bet you're wrong. Not because you're casual with other people's hearts, but because you don't have any idea how beautiful you are. You leave this wake behind you." He turned away from her. "Your book, your paintings, and you. You have no idea what kind of impression you make on people, even my nephew. And Joshua. And Leah. And . . . me."

He looked back at her, his eyes twinkling in the sparkling lights, and no sign of a smile or a joke on his face. She didn't know what to say, so she just looked back at him, wishing he would look away because she couldn't. In the long run, this didn't matter. He might become one of those crushes she wondered about, but nothing more.

Chris August finished up his song of praise, and in its place came the unmistakable accordion notes of the Chicken Dance polka. She laughed out loud.

Gage smiled too. Then he shook a finger at her as he stood up. "I told you, you're on your own. I own this dance." With that he leaped over the railing and ran into the forming circle with his arms up in victory. Meg hesitated, but not for long. She wasn't about to jump the railing, but she made it to the circle of dancers in record time. The circle had grown so big it was larger than the dance floor.

The dancers were better at the chicken part than the polka part, but that just made for more laughter. When she ended up opposite of Gage, she saw him dancing with real chicken skill. She liked the chicken pecking motion he did with his head. That was new. He caught her eye once and stopped to give her a double thumbs up. She was laughing so hard she could hardly keep dancing.

When it was time to polka around the circle, she passed two people and came face to face with Brie. She smiled at her, but Brie breezed past her as if she was invisible. It was pretty easy to tell she had seen her and Gage talking together. Meg tripped over her own feet. She hoped none of this drama was getting back to Leah.

She should stop talking to Gage. If it was going to cause tension, all for some fun conversations and two amazing dances with someone she might never see again, it wasn't worth it. On cue, she ended up one person away from Leah when the final strains of the Chicken Dance sounded. Big wedding dress and all, that girl could shimmy with the best of them. She caught sight of Meg and ran over for a hug, and after a few laughing words Meg had trouble making out, the bride was back in the heart of the dancing again.

If anyone was wondering if the city-girl bride was going to enjoy her mountain wedding, they didn't have to wonder any longer.

Meg got pulled into some silliness when Mark tried his hand at hip-hop. He was terrible. Joshua joined in and was even worse. When the semipros took over the floor, Meg moved on, wiping tears of laughter from her eyes. Standing at the edge of the dance floor waiting for her was Gage, and her decision not to talk to him flew right out of her mind. She took his elbow and they walked back over to the deck. He had two fresh cups of coffee waiting for them.

The coffee was enough to power conversation about Gage's nephew, Meg's upcoming "Say No to Drugs" mural, and the joys and difficulties of working with children. She was surprised to find that Gage had been a sought-after babysitter in his high school years. It made sense, though. She had seen a little of his goofy side, and every child loved to see grownups being goofy.

The battery eventually ran down on the Monster, so

Meg's power station was applied to help start it and buy some more dancing time. The clouds of exhaust from the Hummer as they tried to recharge its battery put a damper on the festivities, even though Caleb turned the Hummer around to send the smoke away from the dance floor. But it was late, and Catherine soon started organizing a convoy of SUVs back to her home. They had to wake up Jacob to get him to start the Expedition.

Gage shook a lot of hands, and Meg got hugs from all of her close relatives and a couple people she didn't quite recognize. Leah and Joshua gave their thanks, and Brie was gracious, but she kept well out of Meg's way. Meg hoped again that Leah didn't notice, but she doubted that was possible. Brie was her best friend. Of course she felt the tension. When Brie climbed into Catherine's car, Meg felt a sense of relief.

Three quarters of the guests left with Jacob and Catherine. The dancers that remained were a determined bunch, but most of the party was over. Leah and Joshua must have finally seen their chance to sneak inside his cabin. Meg felt as if even the deck of the cabin was off limits. It was their wedding night, and she didn't want to intrude. She wondered if Gage had made other arrangements, since it seemed as if his things were still inside the cabin and he hadn't left with Catherine and the others.

"Have you got a place to spend the night?" she asked. By the light of the white Christmas lights she saw the shocked look on his face. She realized her error. "I just wondered. Joshua and Leah, they'll want their privacy. Oh, for heaven's sake, I wasn't inviting you to spend the night in my camper."

He smiled at her discomfort. "Caleb set up a tent for us. I will be sleeping with three men hyped up on lemonade and, possibly, leftover champagne."

"Sounds like a good night's sleep."

He shrugged. "When I'm tired I can sleep through just about anything. I just hope there's no practical joker with shaving cream in the bunch." He reached out for her hand. It sent a thrill through her, but she chided herself. She was way too old to be thrilled by a boy wanting to hold her hand. "You look tired, Meg. Would you like me to walk you back down? I'd take Joshua's truck, but I'm not even sure it will start again."

She didn't want him to offer to walk her back down. She wanted him to insist they go dance beside the cabin again, just the two of them. But she was tired, and he looked tired too, and the night had to end at some point. "I have to get my bag," she said.

He walked her to the table, where a few of the guests' belongings remained, and she found her bag and water bottle. She slung the bag over her shoulder and glanced up to see Gage staring at the grassy spot where they had been dancing. When his eyes turned to her, they were shadowed and impossible to read in the darkness.

Her heart was pounding. The night is over, she reminded herself. She didn't want him to ask her to dance again, because she wouldn't say no. "Ready to head out?" she asked.

He took her elbow. They passed the meadow, and she noticed that some of the light strings were beginning to dim. She stopped and turned. She wanted to remember this—the lights and music in the middle of the forest, on the side of the mountain, in a dead-end valley at the end of rough gravel roads. Then they headed down Joshua's long, steep driveway. Gage didn't ask why she had stopped.

As soon as the road started getting steep, she began to slip. At first she worried about scuffing her shoes, although her feet were sore enough now that she considered throwing them away. Then after a couple close calls, she wondered if she was going to break an ankle or somersault down the road. She laughed at herself. Gage took a firmer grasp of her elbow until she slipped again on the loose gravel and he almost pulled her arm out if its socket trying to keep her upright.

After that, he put one arm around her waist and held on to her other hand in his. It seemed to her that he was holding her hands just like the promenade position from contra dancing the night before. Had it only been one day since then?

"Am I going to have to give you my boots to get you down this mountain?" he teased. Then he slipped himself, nearly taking her down with him.

"Leather soles, eh? Forget it. At least my heels are working a little like cleats." They were deep in the darkness, now, and the starlight and the glow from a moon she couldn't see was their only guide on the road. They giggled and held on to each other, stopping frequently. She imagined they must look like a little old couple, hobbling down the road together.

She heard a sound behind her but ignored it until Gage stopped. He held up one hand to keep her silent. Her eyes strained in the darkness. There it was again, a sound that was something between a breath and a step. He turned to face the sound. When his arm reached back to shove her behind him, Meg was afraid. She wanted to ask him what it was, what he saw. Instead she slowly reached into her bag. Water bottle, sweater . . . where was the flashlight? She felt something cold and hard and grabbed hold.

At that moment Gage threw his hands out. "Don't run, Meg," he said in a low growl. She pulled up what she thought was a flashlight, but it was too big. She had the bear spray. Just as well. She reached into her bag with the other hand as he pushed her backward to the side of the road.

"Get away!" Gage yelled in a deep voice. "Back off, get away! Don't mess with us, we are huge!"

Huge? Meg got the hint. She held the bear-spray hand out, trying to make them look like one large animal. She held out the messenger bag with her other hand. She stared at the darkness that was Gage's back and prayed. *Please, God, keep us safe.* "Bear spray's in my hand," she said.

He jerked backward and she almost tumbled to the ground when he ran into her, but as he spun around to put his arms around her, she got her first glance as the shadow flashed past. She saw the shape, the speed, and a moonlit tail. She couldn't breathe. It was on the run down the driveway now, but the fear wasn't fading. She had been one step away from a mountain lion.

She stood shaking. Gage watched the lion go, then grabbed her by the arm and marched her slipping and tripping down the driveway. When they reached the old logging road, she could finally put words together. "Was it a mountain lion?"

"Yes. A little one."

Little? There was nothing little about it! She had to jog to keep up with Gage. She looked over her shoulder again and again, listening for the sound of cat paws in the dark, but all she could hear was the rustle of their own steps through the tall grass. He reached the camper first and jerked the door open, and she was relieved she hadn't locked it. He half helped, half pushed her inside, then followed and shut the door.

For the one second that they stood there in the dark and quiet of the camper, she realized how hard he was breathing. He had been scared, too. Meg reached for the DC light switch, and comforting light flooded the little camper. Fear was still running through her veins, and she looked around nervously. "He won't come in through the camper, will he? Gage, we have to go up and warn the others!"

"I don't think so." Gage pushed forward until he could sit down at the tiny table. "It was a juvenile, probably out on his own for the first time, looking for his own territory. He was pretty freaked out. And most importantly, he was heading down into the valley. I can't imagine he wants to go back into the chaos up there." He looked at her and his eyes smiled. "Besides, the mean lady with the bear spray might get him."

"Hey! I couldn't tell what it was, bear, human, or whatever." He reached across the table and closed his hand over hers, but she didn't feel any better. "I wasn't prepared. I didn't have any idea what to do."

It was infuriating to look up and see a smile on his face, no matter how kind it was. "It's hard being a planner, isn't it? You spend so much time preparing. You've probably saved people from trouble they'll never even know about. My sister's a planner, so is my mom. What you need is a fixer."

"A *fixer*?"

"A fixer. You don't need another planner; you guys would just be butting heads all the time about how to plan. You need a fixer. So when things fall apart and it looks like you can't pick up the pieces, instead of feeling bad about it, you can step back and let someone else fix it all. Someone who likes challenges a lot more than he likes avoiding them."

She leaned back, pulling her hand with her. "I suppose you know one of these fixers."

"I know a few." Oh, those sparkling amber eyes. "But I still think the kitty wouldn't have liked that bear spray. Besides, we did very well. We looked big and sounded intimidating. Just never let them circle behind you, that's how they kill you."

"What?"

"They bite you on the back of your neck and puncture your spinal cord."

Meg looked at him in horror. "Too much information. And how do you know that? Are there mountain lions in Austin?"

He laughed. "Maybe not in the city. But they're all over the west. Puma, panther, mountain lion—all the same bad kitty. You handle them a little differently than a bear, but I'd be interested to try the bear spray theory out. Maybe when I walk back up I'll get a chance to test it out."

"No!" she said, too loudly. She knew he was teasing her, but she was too scared not to take the bait. "Please don't walk up there alone. You could take my Jeep. No, there's no top on it, the mountain lion could jump right in and get you. I think you should stay a little while, until he's gone."

"I'm sure he's long gone."

Meg didn't answer. The thought of Gage being out there in the dark with that mountain lion was awful. Being alone in her camper with the mountain lion out there wasn't much better.

He must have seen the look in her eyes, because he suddenly changed his tune. "Well, I suppose I could stay a little while. It might set tongues wagging."

"I'd rather face a little gossip than a mountain lion." Her legs were still shaky, so she sat down across the table from him.

"Are you sure?" he asked. "I've been on the tail end of it even more than I deserved, and it can be grim." Then with a look of surprise he noticed the drawings spread across the table. "Are these new?"

"I did them earlier today."

He looked surprised. "Really? All of this? You must work fast." He chuckled at one of the drawings. "Is this for Christmas? Mouse looks like he has Christmas trees on his antlers." He picked up another drawing. "Oh, who's the horse? I like him."

Of course you do. "That's a wild mustang. He hasn't got a name yet."

"And a fox, too. The forest is getting bigger." He glanced up at her. "No mountain lion?"

"No, and there probably never will be! I don't like making scary animals look cute to little kids."

"A moose is pretty scary. A mustang stallion will kill you, too. And if that fox has rabies—"

"I think I know why you don't write children's stories, Gage. No one really wants to read the scene where the bad kitty severs the spinal cord of some innocent forest creature."

Gage laughed long and hard over that one. She liked making him laugh. Finally he said, "Could you draw something tiny for my nephew? Cole would love it."

"What animal does he like best?"

"Well, he likes Mouse the Moose best. Other than that he likes bears, mountain lions, bobcats—"

"I like bobcats. They have fluffy paws and ears."

"They eat happy little forest critters."

She glowered at him and pulled a pencil and the

143

drawing tablet in front of her. She thought for a while. Of course a little boy would like a bobcat. They are small but powerful, and they move silently. And like little boys, they are really cute in a dangerous way. She drew one standing triumphantly, and put one of Gage's sneaky grins on its face, just in case that ran in the family. He was on a rocky ledge, and she drew it as if he was above the viewer. She got up to rummage for her tin of pencils and dug through it for midnight blues. It would have to be nighttime. A golden crescent moon, a few glittering stars. His tan fur would have blue shadows in the nighttime. Claws? No claws. He had a full belly and was only out for fun. Behind him were the black treetops with silver highlights, and an owl silhouetted against the dark blue sky.

The drawing was done, and Meg had no idea how much time she had spent making it. She might have forgotten she wasn't alone, but there was something deeply satisfying in the way Gage concentrated on her drawing the whole time. At the bottom of the drawing she wrote, "Cole the Ninja Bobcat" and signed her name. Then she ripped it off the drawing pad and handed it to Gage. He almost looked afraid to take it from her. "He's going to love this," he said. "It's amazing." All trace of joking was gone.

Meg felt a little embarrassed. "It's not high art," she said.

"Who gets to say what high art is? When I hang something on my wall I'd rather it didn't make me feel depressed, irritated, or scared all day."

"So I shouldn't draw you a mountain lion?"

His eyes lit up. "Would you draw something for me? Really? I don't want to push you, the drawing for Cole is amazing enough."

She smiled. "I like doing it."

"It shows. No mountain lion, though. I want a drawing of the wild mustang . . . if it's not too much to ask, of course. Should I commission you? I mean, I'd be willing to pay."

She kicked him under the table, which wasn't hard because in that tiny space their legs overlapped anyway. "Wild mustang it is." *Of course.*

She stared at the blank paper, but in her mind she was watching a movie. Wild mustang stallion. Nighttime wasn't his time, daytime was. No, sunrise, the beginning of an adventure. Green grass, but instead of eating it, he'd be dancing. How do horses dance? She pictured rodeo bucking horses. No, that wasn't quite right. Racehorses, reining horses, barrel racers, rodeo horses—they were all wrong. She pictured a rodeo bucking horse, but the head down, the desperation, just didn't fit. But jumping did. This mustang would be jumping just for the fun of it. Leaping. Not head down for the balance and force of it, but head up, just enjoying the feel of stretching out long legs, catching the scent of the Montana air.

She sketched the horse coming down between leaps, front hooves together and reaching for the grass, back legs bucking free, head up and tilted, picking a cloud to aim for with his next jump.

"He doesn't look like a planner," Gage asked.

"Very funny."

"Is he alone?" Gage asked. She could hear a little disappointment in his voice.

She looked up at him. "Who would he be hanging out with, a bobcat?" He shook his head. "A fox?" He shook his head again. Good.

"No, another horse. A pretty little mustang mare."

"And what is she doing?"

He stared at her drawing. He seemed to be thinking about it very seriously. "Probably laughing at him," he said. "But not really."

Meg could see that clearly in her mind. She drew another mustang, smaller and rounder, a pale palomino the same color as the famous stallion Cloud in Montana's Pryor Mountains. She was looking at the stallion over her shoulder, pretty mane and tail flowing in the breeze. She didn't want to act like she was impressed by his antics, but she was.

The rest came fast, or at least it seemed that way to Meg. She saw the blue sky with the golden hint of sunrise in the horizon, long blue-green patches of pines bordered by patches of white snow still left in the shadows, wide green meadows with infinite purple lupines. Her favorite memories of seeing the mustangs in the Pryor Mountains came together all in one place, in one image. This was the reason she usually didn't use a camera. The camera never captured things the way she remembered. The stallion was buckskin with a shock of unruly black mane and tail. And just below their hooves, scattered through the green grass, she drew tiny white flowers.

As the drawing came together Meg realized that she had been sitting in one place for a long time, perhaps even hours. Her legs were stiff, and her right shoulder ached. All the while Gage had barely moved. He laughed at the look on the mare's face, oohed over the sunrise, aahed as simple pencil strokes turned into a field of lupines in the distance. "Done," she finally said.

"Sign it."

She did, though she felt self-conscious about it.

"What are you going to call it?"

She thought about that for a while. She wrote "Gage's Mustang" at the bottom. It was vague enough, but she knew what it meant.

He took it from her and set it in front of him, then started to laugh softly. "It's even better right side up," he said. The smile lingered on his face. "I could watch you draw forever."

It was one of the most romantic things she had ever heard.

There wasn't anything she could say. She sat lost in the look of his amber eyes and the warmth of his admiration. She drew silly critters, and he admired her for it. Things didn't get much better than this.

Gage finally broke the silence. He took his drawing, put it next to Cole's, and put them both safely aside. "Tell me what's going on with Mouse and the antler Christmas trees," he said.

They talked for a while about the bones of her story idea. He had lots of questions and even some suggestions. Of the suggestions some were good, some were awful, and all of them made her think. Her mind was buzzing with ideas. But even as they spoke they were trading contagious yawns back and forth across the table. Finally Gage rubbed his eyes and asked, "Have you got any tea? I know I should go. But if you don't kick me out, I don't want to. I'm having too much fun."

This handsome man was having too much fun talking about her children's books characters. Even though she was tired, Meg wasn't ready to call it a night either. She filled a small pan with some drinking water and turned on the burner. Deep in thought about her story, she got lost for a while waiting for the specks on the bottom of the pan to turn into real bubbles. A funny sound made her turn around, and she saw Gage face down on the table. He was deeply asleep, and snoring.

Meg turned off the burner and stared at him. She should wake him up this instant, send him off in her Jeep. She knew that. But instead she watched the rise and fall of his steady breaths under the gabardine jacket. It stretched across his broad shoulders and his long arms. She thought of how it felt to be circled by those arms, dancing to songs older than either of them.

She backed up a few steps and took a fleece throw from her bed. She put it over his shoulders while her mind was saying no, it was past time to wake him up, and who did she think she was tucking him in like a boyfriend—or a husband? No, she reasoned, she'd wake him up in a second. She just didn't want him to get cold in the meantime.

She sat down on the edge of her bed just a couple feet away from him. She wondered why there was so much comfort in his presence. It changed everything. Her book looked brilliant with him around, and her camper was an enviable work of art. She stared at him. Then she flopped back onto her back and thought, *I really don't want him to go back to Texas.*

And that was the last thing she remembered thinking on the night of Joshua and Leah's wedding.

Sunday

Bang bang bang! The old aluminum door of her camper rattled with every strike. Meg's first conscious thought was that the mountain lion was trying to get in. She tried to get up but found herself tangled in blankets. By the time the sound ended she was sitting upright, wondering if she'd been dreaming.

There was a man getting up from her floor, rubbing his wild black hair, wearing a nice wedding jacket that was now quite dusty and half covered with a fleece throw. It was a shocking scene. He caught sight of her, looked confused for a split second, and then gave her that troublesome grin. "Hi," he said. It was all he had time to say before the banging on the camper door resumed.

Meg jumped to her bare feet, but he was faster. Gage went for the door as if it was his camper. "Hold your horses!" he shouted. As he opened it he looked at her and grinned, "Get it? Horses?"

The door flew open, and Joshua stood on the ground below. He glared at Gage, over to Meg, and then back to Gage. "I think you'd better get out here," he said.

Meg couldn't figure out what was going on. Why was Joshua here? Why did he look angry? That creeping guilty feeling came back strongly. She hadn't done anything wrong, had she? Of course she had, she hadn't waked Gage. This looked bad. But why was Joshua here? "Oh no, is it the mountain lion?" she asked. "Did it hurt someone?"

"What mountain lion?" Joshua barked, irritated.

Gage stepped out and she intended to follow, but she was barefoot. She reached for her burgundy shoes, but she couldn't even imagine putting them back on her sore feet. She grabbed the next closest thing, a pair of pink and brown fuzzy slippers. She trotted out of the camper and stopped short.

Her campsite was crowded. Joshua was staring at Gage, his arms crossed over his chest, one fist clenching under his elbow. But that wasn't the worst of it. Walking up was a teary Brie, and with her arm around her, a very cross-looking Leah.

"This must be the worst honeymoon ever," Meg said. She didn't mean to say it out loud, but nerves tended to loosen her tongue.

Gage laughed. Then he pointed at her slippers. "Nice," he said, and gave her a thumbs up.

They were the only ones smiling.

Meg took stock of the situation. First of all, there was Joshua. Unlike her, he had on a clean change of clothes. Since when did he get up early? Maybe it was later than she thought.

Then there was the crying maid of honor. What had happened to her? Meg tried to make sense of it. Brie was glaring at Gage. Meg wondered if Brie had just told Joshua something new and horrible about Gage. Or maybe he had been lying to him. Maybe he was lying to her. Did people who liked drawings of ninja bobcats lie? Meg felt self-doubt closing in on her.

Worst of all was Leah. She was looking at her new husband, and everything about her expression dripped irritation. Meg closed her eyes for a second. If she had ruined Leah's wedding somehow, she would never forgive herself.

"That," said Joshua, pointing at Meg, "is my sister. Well, she's like my sister. And you know that. What are you doing?"

Gage gave Joshua the same patient look he had given Brie the night before. "I know she is, Josh."

Leah was staring at Meg's slippers. Then her dress. Then her face. She scowled and looked back at Joshua, and Meg felt terrible.

"Just answer the question, Gage. What do you think you're doing here?"

Gage's eyes narrowed. So that's what he looks like mad, she thought. He looked calm and dangerous. "Josh, I know you're concerned. I know Meg is family. But you're on the edge of insulting me and her. Are you sure you want to go there?"

"I am there, Gage. On my property, as a matter of fact."

Gage fumed silently. She saw him thinking it over. And as she watched, Meg's mood began to change. Leah being unhappy with her was new and awful, but there was nothing new about Joshua being mad at her. He was right, they had been like brother and sister, and they went through phases where they bickered like crazy. And she hadn't done anything wrong.

So bring it on, she decided. "Joshua Parks, haven't you got something better to do on your first day of married life? It's nice that you care about my welfare, but you forget that I'm twenty-seven and I live an awful lot of my life without your supervision."

He spun on her. "Well, maybe you need it."

Meg felt wounded. This wasn't about what he thought was going on, or whether it was any of his business. Now it was about what kind of person he thought she was and how qualified she was to run her own life. Gage sensed the change in her and his best friend, and he stepped closer to her, almost in front of her. "Josh, you're letting your anger get the best of you. Don't say things you're going to regret."

"The only person around here who doesn't feel regret is you, Gage," Brie said. Her sobs had stopped. She looked furious. "You do whatever you want, and everyone else pays the price."

Leah said something to Brie that Meg couldn't hear, but Brie didn't seem to respond. "Did you think no one would notice you left with her? Did you think no one would notice you didn't spend the night in Caleb's tent? You just thought you'd get away with another conquest?"

Gage took a step forward. "Just hold on a second. There was a mountain—"

"Yep, that's me," Meg said, cutting him off. "Gage's latest conquest. Joshua, I know you're disappointed, deal with it. Leah, I'm sorry about all the turmoil, I hope it stops here. Brie, I don't even know what to say to you, except that if Gage makes you this miserable, you should probably cut the ties and move on." She put one fist on her hips and looked at the watch on her other wrist. "Now I need to get ready for church. Do ya'll mind clearing out?"

Everyone stared at her. It was Leah's eyes she avoided, because she hated having any part of casting a shadow over her wedding. Leah began pushing Brie back down the road. The Monster was there. How had she slept through the sound of that engine? She turned back to Gage, who was the last to move. "I'm going," he said. "You sure you'll be okay?" She nodded. As he walked by, he handed her the fleece throw and threw her a brilliant smile. She smiled back at him, and then he ran to catch up with the others.

Meg wondered if they'd even give him a ride.

She pivoted in her fluffy slippers and got back in her camper trailer. She headed toward the bathroom to brush her teeth and caught sight of herself in the mirror, makeup smudged, mascara running, hair tangled. She was mortified. Then she started to laugh. "Oh my," she said to her reflection. "I did set tongues wagging, didn't I?" She said a little prayer for peace in her family, then started laughing again for no good reason. "I hope you have a 'fixer' handy, Lord. I certainly didn't plan for this."

Meg's irrationally good mood lasted through her shower, through changing clothes into jeans and her prettiest blouse and putting on a touch of makeup. She made sure to wear boots that made hiking the driveway easier. And she made sure she had the bear spray in her bag. At the last second she added her well-worn Bible and headed out.

She had only made it a little way when she saw the print in the soft, sandy soil of the borrow pit next to the driveway. One big paw print. She took out her phone, which she carried despite having it turned off, and took a picture of it next to her Bible for scale. She figured she could look it up on the Internet and figure out how big the cat might have been. Then she turned the phone back off and headed up the road.

What a beautiful day. What amazing sounds, birds singing, a slight ruffle of wind in the trees. It was Sunday. It was the right day to rest. When she crested the hill and the meadow came into view she had a moment of panic, but she chased it away. She wasn't going to let go of her sense of humor. Still, when her brother came over to her, she was happy to find a safe place to land in his smile.

He said hello and then got to the point. "What is going on? There are crying women, angry men, drama, and Aunt Catherine won't tell me anything."

Meg wouldn't talk. Nope, not now, not this morning. "Sounds exciting. Is there still breakfast?"

"A ton of it. And you don't have coffee in your hand. I can't believe you're smiling without it."

Meg laughed. But coffee sounded good, and they both headed over toward the breakfast tables to get a cup. Last night's dance floor had been packed up, and the compressed grass was trying valiantly to spring back. She glanced around—no sign of Leah or Brie. Was that Gage and Caleb playing football across the meadow? She was happy to see that. It gave her hope for cooler heads and less tongue wagging.

She felt a hand on her shoulder and looked up into Catherine's eyes. "Are you okay?" the older woman asked.

Meg smiled. "I am, thanks."

"Is something wrong?" Mark asked.

Catherine shooed him away. "Silly girl stuff, Mark. Meg, have you had breakfast yet? You should get a plate. Jeffrey's service will be starting in about fifteen minutes." With that Catherine went back to dishing out eggs and sausage to grateful and hungry guests. Meg was off the hook—another pleasant surprise.

Then Leah appeared on the deck and crooked a finger at Meg. Meg's good mood sank in an instant. Leah looked downright mad.

Holding her coffee and breakfast because she had no idea where to set it down, Meg walked up onto the deck like it was the plank on a pirate ship. Leah crooked her finger again, indicating that Meg had to walk all the way across the deck to the corner where she stood. It felt like climbing a mountain. When she got there Leah crossed her arms and scowled. "I can't tell you how mad I am about all of this."

She was so mad that her southern twang was coming out, making 'mad' a two-syllable word. It sounded cute. Meg braced herself. "I'm sorry, Leah," she said.

"I mean, all this silliness, and every single bit of it could have been avoided. There are a lot more important things to be thinking about on the morning of the Sabbath. And to have friends, and even family now, behaving so badly . . . well, it's a mess."

Meg didn't speak. She refused to defend herself. If Leah wanted to vent, she would let her.

"I mean, first Brie acts like a love-struck pup all over again, and then she gets to gossiping about you, and just when Joshua should have told her to stuff it, she starts crying. I swear, that man can't handle a woman crying. If I ever want a new car, I guess all I'll have to do is get a couple tears in my eyes and he'll go sell our firstborn son for the down payment."

Meg was completely lost. She didn't know what was coming next. When some of her scalding hot coffee dripped over her hand, she had the presence of mind to set her breakfast down on a nearby table.

Leah shook her head briskly. "What a mess. It's nobody's business what you do or what you don't do. I hope you'll forgive Josh for this, Meg. Brie got him all worked up. She knows how much honor and family mean to him, and she made it sound like Gage was after you."

After me? Meg wondered what that meant. She reminded herself that it was thirdhand information, and it could mean anything. She knew better than to dwell on it.

"If it helps any, Meg, I want you to know that you handled all this mess just right. You took the wind out of everyone's sails. Even Brie's, and she's been nursing this bitterness for a long time. Now they'll have an hour with God to think about it. You haven't even eaten. Here, let's sit down."

Meg was still in shock, but she did as she was told. "I'm still sorry, Leah."

Leah giggled. "Oh honey, I'm the one who's sorry. I could tell by the look on your poor face this had to be the worst morning ever. How unfair, since you're the one who taught me the best way to wake up Joshua—coffee and if necessary a pillow. By the way, I'm glad you finally changed clothes," she said with a wink. "I didn't point it out to Joshua that you were clearly wearing the same clothes you wore last night. When I heard what you said about being Gage's latest conquest—that was rich!—I knew right then that they all needed to sit with that for a while. Joshua needs to think about what's his business and what isn't, and Brie needs to think about Gage. Gage will probably just think about you. I think shutting up for an hour-long church service ought to sort it all out."

Leah was definitely a fixer, Meg thought. She silently thanked God for sending her one, just like she'd asked.

"When Gage and I walked down last night we ran into a mountain lion," Meg said. "He ran away, down toward the valley, but I was pretty scared. And I didn't want Gage walking out there, or even driving my Jeep, with its plastic walls. So we talked. And it was really, really nice."

Leah demanded details about the mountain lion, and after she got over the shock of it, she laughed along with Meg about whether or not she could have fended it off with bear spray. Then she said, "I'm really glad Gage was there for you."

Meg took another sip of coffee while she worked up courage to ask what she wanted to ask. "Are you sure? Because it seems as if you've had mixed feelings about him. And your opinion matters to me, Leah."

Leah frowned. "I did give you mixed messages. I was mistaken about something then. I didn't want to gossip, Meg, but I think I did. I don't know if saying what I know now would be any better. It's expecting two wrongs to make a right, isn't it? So I'm just going to talk about me. I thought Gage's treatment of Brie was misleading. Now I don't. If you want to know more, I think you should talk to him."

"That's fair." And way too intriguing. She glanced over her shoulder to find that Gage was still playing football across the meadow. He was wearing a button-down shirt and khakis and had switched into sneakers. Meg missed the rose-decorated boots.

No matter what he was wearing, he was a handsome man. She got a little distracted watching him stretch out to catch the ball, long arms extended in midair, like some sort of eagle. When she looked back at Leah, the new bride was shaking her head. "You've got it bad."

"I do not! I just met him. Rats. What gives it away?"

Sonya started calling people over to the center of the meadow, where the wedding ceremony had been. "Bring a chair!" she was calling, so Leah and Meg each carried over one of the lighter chairs from the deck. Everyone else was still milling around. Where was Joshua? Or Brie? Leah seemed unperturbed by their absence. Meg reminded herself that she was in a good mood, and until she learned otherwise, she was not God's appointed fixer today. Besides, an hour-long church service would do her some good, too.

Leah set her chair down near where Jeffrey and Sonya were standing, and she motioned for Meg to sit next to her. People started planting chairs in patches all around them. Meg opted for another cup of coffee and hurried over to get her bag and her empty cup for a refill, and when she came back she found Joshua sitting next to Leah and Gage pulling up a chair next to Meg's empty chair. None of them appeared to be speaking, or even looking, at the other two. How cozy, Meg thought, and then reminded herself again about her good mood. And she was in a good mood. It was beautiful, Josh and Leah were successfully married even if they were a little cranky at the moment, and she had one more day off work.

And Gage thought her drawings were beautiful.

So she sipped her coffee, settled in, and put her mind on God instead of them. Or Catherine sitting behind her. Or the bee flying over Sonya's head. Nothing but sunlight and God. "It is Sunday," she sighed with relief. Out of the corner of her eye she saw three sets of eyes turn to her. She ignored them all and tried not to laugh. It was good, knowing that whatever irritation Josh and Leah felt, they were family. And so was she. It would all work out, like it had countless times before. And Gage? Well, he was on his way back to Texas today. That was out of her control. God hadn't made her a fixer anyway.

It felt nice to have him sitting next to her. When she

decided to sneak a glance, he was looking right at her, and he winked. She just about spilled her coffee again.

Sonya was handing out sheets of paper, and Meg got one as they passed the stack around. It was a list of lyrics for contemporary worship songs. One of the better guitarists was pulling up a set next to Uncle Jeffrey, who was good in his own right. Meg had a very mediocre voice, but that didn't matter. She loved this part. She set her coffee cup on the grass and stood up along with the others. God made her voice, so he probably didn't mind the sharp notes and, once in a while, inadvertent yodeling.

Music always helped her concentrate on why she was there. It was to ponder God, and to be grateful, and to let all of the rest of her life fall back into its rightful place. Funny how many things slid down her list of priorities when she took time to think about it on a Sunday.

She sat down again with the others after two songs and reached down for her cup of coffee. Just beneath it she caught three tiny white flowers starting to open. There weren't any others near her feet, although she glanced around. Just three under her Styrofoam coffee cup. She glanced up at Gage and found him smiling at her. "What?" she mouthed.

"You're cute," he whispered.

He must like yodeling, she thought.

Jeffrey handed his guitar to his wife and pulled out a well-worn Bible. It looked dog-eared, sticky noted, and stained. As she took her own out of her bag she wondered if Bible abuse ran in the family.

"Since weddings are on everyone's mind today," Jeffrey began, "we're going to start today with something that probably sounds familiar. It's the stuff that wall plaques and posters are made of. I've even seen it attributed to 'Anonymous' on a T-shirt.

"As it turns out, this saying is actually the word of God, and you can find it in 1 Corinthians 13:4-5. I'd like these words to sink in for a moment, so if you can, listen like it's all brand new. 'Love is patient, love is kind. It does not envy, it does not boast, it is not proud. It does not dishonor others, it is not self-seeking, it is not easily angered, it keeps no record of wrongs.'"

Jeffrey talked about how hard it is to be married for years and not end up with some sort of tally in the back of your mind. He reminded everyone that if you have a list, you can be sure your spouse has one too, and the chances of either of you making up for the items on that list were slim to none.

The sermon was about having faith in love. Meg knew that was one of the things that had kept her from getting too close to some of her suitors. Maybe she hadn't had enough faith in her family's love, either. She always knew they loved her, but she had always felt like she was one wrong move from losing that love.

She wasn't the missionary her parents wanted to be. And she wasn't Catherine's blood daughter. But their love stayed, imperfect but enduring. Maybe she could learn to have faith in that. And that was probably part of the reason for her good mood. She threw Joshua, her un-brother, a big smile. He looked confused, and she thought that was funny.

"The problem is that some marriages dissolve into a season where only the bad things get through. 'I like your shirt' begins to sound like 'You're stupid,' and "I want to have another kid' sounds like 'You don't support our family.' Being easily angered means that you are off track. And as with most derailments, it's easiest to fix if you stop before all the wheels are off.

"Besides, it's funny how God manages to match us up so someone's able to do the important stuff, according to what He thinks is important," Jeffrey was saying.

"One of you will be a good dishwasher. One of you will remember to change the oil. One of you will be better at paying bills, and the other one is probably better at finding the right Christmas presents. These things are gifts. You can't buy them, you can't expect them, and you get what you get. And even when it's annoying, we should be grateful. And you know it can be annoying."

There was a small ruffle of laughter through the congregation. To her right Leah and Joshua exchanged a couple whispered words and Leah giggled.

Just then Gage leaned over. "See? You need a fixer."

Jeffrey boomed on. "As a matter of fact, love is about building up the other person. If you have a deep need, a real and persistent need, then I suggest you turn to God to fill it up. He's the only one who can fix it."

She glanced at Gage. He raised one eyebrow and whispered, "Ha ha. God's on my team."

"What's even better than that," Jeffrey added, "is that God has a plan for you. You can hope, and expect, that plan to bring you what you really need, not just the things that you want. And that includes your spouse."

She turned to Gage. "Go Team Planners," she whispered.

From somewhere behind her she heard Catherine's distinctive, short "Shhh."

Meg pulled herself back together before she started laughing. A good mood was great, but a full-on preteen giggle fit would be embarrassing. She'd had enough embarrassing moments for one morning.

"Of course this scripture does remind us of marriage, especially after a sweet night like last night. But for some of you, weddings bring up a lot of unwelcome thoughts. You may be remembering the early days of a relationship when things looked so promising, before things went wrong."

Old heartaches rose up in Meg's chest, and she thought of Brie. Feeling that bad can make it hard to move on. It might even make a girl, a nice and loving girl, act badly.

Jeffrey took a couple steps forward into the crowd of mismatched chairs. "Marriage without the covenant, whether you actually bothered to go through a ceremony or not, is bound to break your heart. It can leave you with so much scar tissue that it's hard to touch your heart at all anymore."

The crowd was very quiet. For all his casual style, there was something convicting about a pastor making eye contact with you when he was talking about sex and marriage.

Meg sat very still and hoped he wouldn't look at her. But he did, just when he started to speak again. "I spoke to a young man recently who had broken his own heart. I know that sounds funny, but that's what happened. He had been too casual with his own heart, and the hearts of several young women."

She felt a brush against her hand. Gage was staring intently at Jeffrey, but he was reaching for her hand. She took it, realizing that Jeffrey might be talking about Gage. She felt like she needed to brace herself for what he would say.

"This young man did a good job of giving up his self-seeking ways. But he had also given up on love." Jeffrey took a step back and looked away, and Meg breathed again. "When he met a young woman he really cared for, he didn't know how to act. Think about it. How many good examples do you have for how to properly court or be courted? Do you even know the difference between dating and courting? Let me tell you the difference. If your grandparents are still married, they probably courted."

Meg's mind was on fire. She was trying so hard not to think it, but the more she pushed it down the more it bobbed to the top: If the pastor was talking about Gage, could she be the woman Gage had met, the one he cared for?

"So that brings me to the last part of this scripture, the part that is important for young men like the one I was talking about, and all the young women who would want to be courted. The word is patience. Love is patient. Being kind takes patience. Being discerning takes patience. If it's not the right relationship, be patient with God to send you the right person in His own perfect time."

Gage's hand stayed tight on hers.

Jeffrey grinned. "If you're losing hope, take a good look at Josh and Leah, who found each other at just the right time. To hear Josh tell it, he knew the very second he saw Leah that she was the one. That doesn't mean he threw discernment out the window.

"But from day one Joshua treated Leah as if she could be the faithful, loving, Godly wife he hoped for. So here's my challenge to each of you. If you are, were, or think you might fall in love, take one week to treat your boyfriend or girlfriend like they are Godly, loving, faithful, patient, and kind. See if love grows. And if it doesn't, you might want to dump them."

Laughter again. To Meg some of that laughter sounded forced, though.

"Whatever you do, don't close off that space in your heart. God has a plan for it. Shall we pray?"

Meg bowed her head and closed her eyes, and she listened to her uncle's heartfelt prayer. Her brother Mark was going to be like him, blunt, insightful, and patient. She was sure he was on the right track with his new job and school. *One more thing I don't need to fix, Lord. You've got a plan.*

She peeked down to look at Gage's hand enclosing her own. What a wonder that was, how natural it felt, and how comforting. And sexy. Yep, just his skin against hers, palm to palm, was enough to make her heart race. It probably wasn't the kind of thing to think about during prayer, she reminded herself. She hadn't thought about marriage for a long time, and here she was, letting her mind wander that way with a man she hardly knew, thanks to Gage's handsome self and Uncle Jeffrey's sermon.

A chorus of "Amen" brought her back to reality, but before she raised her head, she prayed her own silent prayer. Okay, I'll give it a try for one week. And when it doesn't work out, I will dump him, if he doesn't dump me first. Of course he'll be in Texas, but that's one of those pesky details you're going to have to work out, God.

They got to sing again. That was when she noticed that Gage sang well but not perfectly. She thought he was pretty cute, too.

When the service was over she picked up her messenger bag, and while she was looking down she was nearly tackled by her cousin. "I was an idiot this morning," Joshua said. "I'm sorry. I got all worked up and acted like a jerk." He pulled back and looked at Gage. "I owe you the biggest apology, my friend."

Next to him, Leah cleared her throat.

"Okay, after my wife I owe you the biggest apology. I know better. I got caught up in all sorts of nonsense, and I know better. I know it! I just thought—"

Gage cut him off with a back-thumping hug that Meg scrambled to avoid before she got a black eye. "No problem. It was actually pretty funny. I feel sorry for any guy who tries to date your daughter, Josh. Besides, you hadn't had any coffee yet, you can't be held accountable for your actions."

"Really?" Meg said. "You woke up *before* you drank your coffee?"

"Well, I didn't exactly wake up, I was already awake because—"

Leah kicked him in the ankle.

"Uh, yes. I woke up before I drank any coffee."

Beside her she felt Gage's hand sneak into her own again. It made the color rise in her face, and she tried to keep her smile even. He cared for her. The conversation went on to more neutral topics, and Meg finally worked up the courage to look Gage in the eye.

His amber eyes were sparkling. Meg didn't think she'd ever had a man look at her like that before. It sent warmth and sunshine all the way down into her soul.

Leah's laugh startled her, and she turned away and tried to catch up to the conversation topic, but her mind was elsewhere. It was on the tall Texan. He might not be the "real cowboy" she had been looking for as a girl, but she had been so right to want to look in Texas!

As she was trying to gather her thoughts, she caught sight of Brie headed their way. She looked perfect, perfect hair and makeup, but she also looked sad. Meg's heart went out to her. She gave Gage's hand a squeeze and said, "I need to find my parents. I'll be back." Brie wouldn't want her hanging around for whatever she was planning to say.

Meg found her parents talking to Mark. The four of them stood in the sunshine and talked for a while about Mark's plans. Now that she was getting used to the idea of him becoming a pastor, she could see his excitement shining though. Her parents talked about the church tour they would be starting next Sunday to drum up support for their mission work. Then Meg's mother put her hand on her arm and said, "Honey, Catherine gave me one of your books. It is lovely. I laughed so hard! I know kids must love it, but I bet their parents do, too. I can't wait to read your next one. Is it done yet?"

"No," she answered. But the hardest part was done— having an idea worth pursuing. "Thanks, Mom."

As the conversation went on, she glanced down at their shoes. Four pairs of practical shoes. They all stood the same way, too, with toes pointing slightly outward. On the dark, trampled grass, their feet made a four-pointed star. This is my family, she thought, and it made her heart swell. It was different from other people's families, it wasn't as close as many, but it was hers, and they were linked in ways that couldn't be broken.

Meg promised to hold on to that image, four pairs of boots making a star. She needed to remind herself to be grateful for how much love there was in her life.

Glancing over her shoulder, she could see that Leah and Joshua had moved on, but Gage stood in the same spot talking to Brie. She seemed to be dabbing at a tear in her eye, and he reached out to put his hand on her shoulder. Meg looked away. She didn't want to be seen. This was their business, not hers, and no matter what, she hoped it could be resolved.

Meg heard the sound of a car starting up, and she turned to see one car pulling out and people loading up at least three more. The wedding was over, the free food had been eaten, and it was time to go home. Meg felt a sense of urgency. How much time did she have left with Gage? She was only just beginning to know him.

"Thanks, Mark," her father said. "Jacob was going to drive us down when he took some people to the airport, but it would have been very crowded."

"The airport? Do you know who he's taking?" She tried to sound only mildly interested, but her brother gave her a quizzical look.

"Leah and Joshua's friends, I think. They're both flying out to . . . where are they from again?"

"Texas," Meg supplied. Bozeman wasn't the biggest airport in the world. There might be only one flight that would connect to Austin going out today, so of course they would be flying together. "Do you know when they're leaving?"

"In about half an hour," her mother said. She touched Meg's arm again, gently.

Everyone gave her a patient, slightly sad look. Meg felt as though she had "I Like the Best Man" written across her forehead. "Well," she said brightly, "I'll be leaving about the same time. I want to get down to the KOA before dinnertime. I heard they have an amazing fried chicken dinner at the diner up there." Pat, pat, pat went her mother's hand on her arm.

Another car started, and she turned to see Catherine and Jacob's Expedition start up and move closer to the cabin. Jacob shut it off and got out. To the left of it Gage and Brie were still talking, but now they were walking slowly away. Back at the SUV, Jacob opened the rear door and Joshua loaded a bag into the back. Up on the deck, Leah spotted her and waved for her to come over. Meg gave her parents and her brother an extra hug for no good reason and went back up to join Leah.

Leah was motioning her to come into the cabin. "I just hate it when brides open up their presents in front of everybody. It always felt like the queen was demanding tithes, and everyone just compares their presents to everyone else's," she was saying as she opened the door. "So I didn't. But there's one exception. I really want to make sure I open up your present before you go, because I know it's a painting. I hope it's one of yours. Is it a moose?"

Meg laughed. She thought that would have been a terrible wedding present, but the look in Leah's eyes was so eager. Meg thought she could have painted a stop sign and Leah would have been happy to have it. She felt sorry for Brie, going back to Texas and knowing she'd never have her sweet friend close by again. "No moose," she said. She reconsidered. "Okay, maybe a hint of one."

The cabin door opened and her cousin and Gage came in. They both smiled, and Meg felt her heart thump again. Good grief, she was a mess around that man.

"Come on over, Josh," Leah called, "I'm going to open up Meg's present." She took her time taking the paper off neatly, not tearing a single piece. Meg watched Joshua, and she saw him step forward, stop, and then cross his arms. She knew Joshua was working hard not to tear it out of her hands and rip it to pieces. He had absolutely hated it when Meg had opened her birthday presents the same way. His own birthdays often resembled a tornado.

The painting was of the cabin. Everyone had heard

the story of Leah's first night there. Her cousin and his then girlfriend were snowed in after a Christmas tree hunt. Leah was alone in the cabin when it got dark, and by the time Joshua got back he was worried she'd be frozen half to death. Instead, she'd not only gotten the persnickety old wood-burning stove going, but she'd made a cup of hot chocolate and gotten cozy. Joshua was so surprised to see his city girl girlfriend all comfortable in his remote cabin that he blurted out a proposal rather than waiting for Christmas Eve like he'd planned.

Meg had heard all about it, and that's what she had painted, sort of. She had painted the cabin in snow, Leah standing on the deck with a smile on her face, a quilt around her shoulders, and a steaming mug in her hand. She had painted it from her heart. It was in her own style, a mixture of illustrating she did for children's paintings and her own recollections of this place. She had painted it the way she would have done a painting for herself, in the brilliant, shimmering colors she saw when she looked at the world. When it was revealed, no one said a thing.

"Oh, Meg," Leah said at last. When she turned around she had tears in her eyes. Meg felt so gratified she could hardly breathe. Then Joshua blindsided her with a gigantic hug. A moment later Leah joined in, make it a three-way hug.

When Gage said, "I'm feeling a little left out," the three of them practically tackled him as a joke. He cried uncle, and while the boys continued to push each other around like teenagers, Leah took Meg by the hand and thanked her again.

It was Gage who put the damper on the moment. "So is the bus leaving soon?" he asked Joshua.

"In about twenty minutes."

"I left the drawings in your camper," he said to Meg. "Do you mind if I pick them up?"

She tried to look cheerful. "I can go down now and get them."

"I'd like to walk you down," he said, just as she hoped he would. Joshua said he would have his father stop for Gage at the turnoff for the old logging road, which bought them a few more minutes. But it also meant that Gage had to say his good-byes. He gave Josh a hug and then pushed him again for good measure. Leah was still teary. "See you soon," she said, and he nodded.

See you soon? Leah was even more optimistic than Meg had thought. She was fairly certain the newlyweds wouldn't be going back to Texas anytime soon.

Gage reached for Meg's hand and led her out of the cabin. He didn't let go of it as they walked silently across the meadow, past other guests loading up cars, and down the road. It was hot. Jeans had felt like a good choice in the cool morning, but not now. She could hear cicadas buzzing in the trees, and that even *sounded* hot. The shade of the forest felt good when they reached it. When one of the cars passed them, arms waving good-bye that could have belonged to just about anyone, Gage pulled her aside and looked at her. "I wish I didn't have to go right away," he said.

She nodded. "Back to work in Texas?"

"Just back to packing," he said, leading her out onto the steep dirt road again. The lug soles on her boots handled it much better than her high heels had the night before.

"I have a few leads on places to live," he said, "but nothing better than that. My sister is going to let me fill up her garage with my junk for a little while, which helps."

Meg nodded again. She really didn't want him to talk about moving, because no matter where he was going, it was very far away. And every step they took was closer to the Expedition driving down to take him away.

"I want you to know that I did the best I knew how with Brie," he said. "I wanted to make it up to her. I don't think it's all about me. I think that when I started trying to do right by her, it was the first time she'd ever had a man treat her well."

"Maybe she thought you were the only one who ever would," Meg murmured. And there Meg was, surrounded by men who did right by their family.

"Exactly. But she'll figure it out. Besides, I always annoyed her. She said it was like dating a kid sometimes."

Meg grinned. "I can understand that. I know I'd rather you never parked my camper again."

He looked shocked. "What?"

"Never mind." It didn't matter. In hindsight it was almost funny. The turnoff to the logging road came up sooner than she could have imagined.

"I wanted to ask you a favor," Gage said. "It's a big one, but it would mean a lot to me. Do you think you could let my nephew Cole see your camper sometime?"

Meg doubted that would ever work out. "Of course. But I don't see any way I'd be driving it down to Texas. In fact, I kind of doubt the camper, or my Jeep, could even make the trip." She opened the door and stepped up into the camper, but she felt Gage stop behind her. She turned to see a confused look on his face. Was he trying to invite her to come visit? If so, she was handling it badly. But it was the truth, the camper wasn't made for long trips. *Step out in faith. That doesn't mean stepping all the way to Texas, does it?* She didn't think that was what God wanted her to do. Or Uncle Jeffrey. That would be one big leap of faith, and not a very discerning one, at that.

"But my sister lives in Livingston."

"Livingston?"

"Livingston, Montana."

"Montana?"

He nodded.

Meg's mind was buzzing. "Your sister lives in Montana?"

Gage nodded again, and looked at her like she was a little crazy.

"You're moving to Montana?"

He began to grin.

"Wait, you grew up in Montana, not Texas?"

"Well, yes, I'm from Montana. Sorry, I know that doesn't qualify me to be your Texas cowboy dream come true, but—"

Meg took a leap of faith right out of the camper and into his arms. Luckily Gage was plenty strong enough to catch her, and when she kissed him, he kissed her right back. When he finally let her slide back down to the ground and stopped kissing her, she felt lightheaded.

"What was that for?" he said, looking as if any reason at all would be fine with him.

"I thought you were from Texas, and so your sister was too, so when you said you were moving to be nearer to her I thought . . ."

His eyes grew wide, and then his smile did the same. "You thought . . . ha, Mouse Girl. The joke's on you. I'll be back in Montana in about two weeks. Sooner, if I can pull it off."

Being patient and hopeful looked a lot easier all of a

sudden. "You should take Cole camping in the trailer before the end of the summer," she said. He could drive it like he stole it, for all she cared. He was moving to Montana!

She jumped into her trailer, grabbed his mustang and bobcat drawings, and hopped back out to hand them to him. He looked at her giddy expression and said, "I think I'd better kiss you again." And that was what they were doing when the car horn sounded from the end of the old logging road. Gage looked at her, looked down the road, and then gave her a look that was full of regret. "Meg, I don't want to go, but . . ."

Meg smiled. "Thanks for being my best man," she said. "I'll see you soon." *See you soon.* That was what Leah had meant!

With a bow Gage said, "Thanks for being my maid of honor, Margaret Parks." There was that grin again, the invitation to better things to come.

Mother/Daughter Book Club Questions

1. Meg's art is her joy and her job. What do you think she had to accomplish to get that job? If you wanted to make money doing what you love, what would your job be, and what might it cost you to get it?

2. Gage is a male lead who has treated woman dishonorably in the past. Do you think people can make big changes in their life? How? Do big changes take time to stick? Should Meg trust Gage? Why or why not?

3. Meg's relationship with her mother is strained. Does her mother and father's missionary work play a role in that? How do you think parents should balance their missionary work and family responsibilities? Is the same true if a child feels called to a mission?

4. Meg's cousin Joshua is protective of her when it comes to dating. Do you think he is helpful to her or not? What role does her father play? What role do you think a Christian man should play in his family's "love life," if any?

5. Brie has the kind of looks and style that stand out in a crowd. Do you think Meg stands out in a crowd? From what you learned in the book, what did Gage find attractive about Meg?

6. Do you think Meg and Gage are in love, or is it too soon to tell? How do you know when it's love? Have you ever been wrong?

7. Out of all the characters in the book, who do you think is doing the best job of living a life that brings glory to God? Why? What can you do to encourage each other to do the same?

Acknowledgements

To my husband and kids, thank you for your patience, encouragement, and for teaching me every single day that love is funny, unexpected, glorious, sometimes hard, and always a blessing from God.

Other books by Cynthia Bruner

Fount – Stories of Storms and Grace
- With Amy K. Maddox
and Karin Kaufman

Mountain Duet – Mystery & Romance in the Rockies
- With Karin Kaufman

About the Author

Cynthia Bruner is an inspirational romance author and fine art landscape photographer for whom living in Montana is an endless source of romance, beauty, and humor. To learn more about the Montana Weekend Novella series or other writings, please visit the <u>Montana Inspired Arts</u> (www.montanainspiredarts.com) website.

Made in the USA
Coppell, TX
14 July 2020